The Boy Next Door
An If You Can Prequel Novella
Cheryl Terra

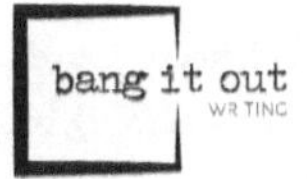

Bang It Out Writing

Author's Note

THIS BOOK IS A prequel to the If You Can series, which follows Nellie Belanger, an unapologetically sensual college student, on her journey from bed to bed. This series features multiple love interests/sexual partners in non-cheating scenarios and has a guaranteed series HEA. Kiss Me If You Can is the first book in the series and takes place three years after the events of The Boy Next Door. It will be released on April 12, 2024.

The If You Can series is loosely based on a collection of short stories. If you have previously read these stories, please note that this is *not* a continuation of that collection. It's more of a reboot than a rewrite, so think more along the lines of some kind of multiple universe situation where the characters have the same names, but even though a new actor is playing the lead role, it's still Spiderm—I mean, Nellie. We're in the Nellie-Verse, if you will.

Please note that this books is written in Canadian English, which has rules and spellings from both UK and US English. It also contains phrases and words specifically from Québécois French. Translations of those can be found at the end of the book.

Content Warning

I have tried to reflect any potential triggers here as best I can without providing spoilers, but if you have concerns about any of the items listed or wish to know more, please reach out to me via email at **info@cherylterra.com**.

Themes + Plot Points: Slut shaming, rumour-spreading, divorce, toxic parenting/familial relationships, large age gaps, lying/secret-keeping all occur within the text. There is a brief mention of an off-screen teenage pregnancy.

SA + Consent: No SA occurs on-page, however jokes are made about non-consensual activity. This is not presented in a positive light and is addressed immediately. There is a situation in this book where consent could be considered questionable based on information being withheld. A brief discussion about a rumour about an off-screen character experiencing birth control tampering occurs.

Spice Variety: Characters in this book and throughout this series will engage in casual hook-ups that may include characters not involved in the main relationship dynamic. This will not include cheating or adultery of any kind between the main characters.

Other: there are moderate mentions of alcohol and drug use

Prologue
Stranger Danger

I WAS ANKLE-DEEP IN mud when I decided I was done with men.

"I'm done with men!" I declared, throwing my hands up.

Across the yard, my dad's mouth tightened into a thin line. Beside him, a man I didn't recognize raised his eyebrows, though he looked amused. Beside *him*, a woman holding a baby pressed her free hand to her mouth, trying to hide her smile.

And my mom, who was halfway across the driveway after bolting towards me, nearly tripped on her own two feet as she dissolved into laughter.

Which, to my four-year-old self, was the ultimate betrayal.

I glared at my mom, putting my hands on my hips. "Why are you laughing at me?"

"I'm not," she said, still laughing as she recovered and jogged towards me, the flowy fabric of her gauzy kimono-style cardigan fanning out behind her. "I'm not, honey."

I looked at my new best friend, Anne-Marie. She was staring at my feet with horror in her eyes and didn't see my incredulous expression of "Can you *believe* this?" But I was looking for *someone* to share my reaction, so I looked up at my dad.

He pressed his lips together harder, though when the man beside him started laughing, his face relaxed and a soft chuckle left his lips.

"You're all laughing at me," I said as my mom reached me.

"We're not," she said.

"You're *still* laughing!" My voice pitched up. "He ruined my shoes and you're *laughing*!"

"They're not ruined, Nellie." She hunched over and put her hands beneath my armpits, huffing as she yanked me out of the mud and set me on the walkway. "We'll wash them off and they'll be perfectly fine."

Which I knew was a *lie*. There was no way my beautiful shoes would ever be the same.

And I hadn't even worn them to school yet. My first day of kindergarten was in a few weeks, and despite the fact that my dad said he could ask his assistant to purchase my supplies and clothes, my mom had insisted on us going shopping together.

"It's what normal families do," she'd said as she tied my shoelaces so we could leave that morning.

"We are a normal family," my dad had responded.

"Yes, but I mean normal as in *normal*." She'd folded her arms. "We're going to Walmart."

He'd sighed. "Fine. Are you ready, then?"

My mom straightened up and grabbed her purse. "I was born ready."

So we'd gone out shopping, first to Walmart and then to a bunch of other stores to get clothes and pencil crayons and a lunch box and the most perfect pair of hot pink and white glitter light-up sneakers that I'd begged and pleaded to wear out of the store until my dad ruffled my hair and agreed, much to my mom's dismay.

We had turned down our street to go home when my dad cursed in French, which he thought I didn't understand, but I knew enough of it to know that *tabarnak* was a very, very bad word.

"Who is blocking our driveway?" he'd snapped.

"Based on context clues, I'm going to guess our new neighbours," my mom said.

"They are not making a very good impression if they think that's an appropriate place for the moving truck."

"Max, they might not even be there yet," my mom said tiredly. "They probably hired movers."

"Of course," he said. "And is it also Bring Your Child To Work Day?"

"What?"

He parked his car on the street outside our house and motioned out the windshield. "*That* does not look like a mover to me."

They kept squabbling, which was frustrating because I very much wanted to know what was going on and couldn't see out the front window. But my dad tended to get annoyed when I interrupted adult conversations, so I stewed silently until I couldn't stand it anymore.

Which was probably, like, ten seconds. But I *did* try.

Then I did something my parents didn't know I could do, which was unbuckle myself from my car seat, slide out of it, and open the car door. It wasn't until I hopped out that my mom whirled around.

"What the *fuck*—" she yelped. "Nellie!"

"Vicki!" my dad said. "Language!"

"My God, I'm *done* with men," she snapped. "She got out of the fucking car, Max! Why don't you have the child locks on the fucking *doors*?!"

She raced out of the car, but by that point, I'd already stomped halfway across the driveway towards the stretch of grass between my house and the one next door, where a girl about my age was sitting.

"*Excuse* me," I said loudly once I was close enough. "Why are you on my grass?"

The little girl looked up, bright brown eyes wide beneath a fringe of dark brown hair. She had white skin with freckles dotted across her nose, round pink cheeks, and thin, haphazard braids in random places all over her head.

"It's your grass?" she asked.

"Yes," I said.

It was not, actually, but neither of us knew that.

"Oh," she said. "Well, if I give you a makeover, can I keep playing here?"

I frowned. "A makeover?"

She held up a strange-looking toy. Without a word, she hooked it around some of her loose hair, then pressed a button. It whirred and after a few moments of what was obviously witchcraft, she pulled it away to reveal she'd added another braid to her hair, this one with tinsel and a feather sticking out of it.

"See?" she said.

"Nellie!" my mom gasped as she rushed up. "Honey, you can't get out of the car like that."

I looked up at her, confused. "Yes, I can."

"*No*, you—"

"But I *did*."

She took a breath and let it out. "You are not supposed to get out of the car like that. You need to wait for Mommy or Daddy to unbuckle your seat."

"Why?"

"If you did that while the car was moving—"

"Mommy, I'm not stupid," I said. "I can't do that when the car is *moving*."

The little girl sitting on the lawn looked up, her round eyes even rounder. "Did you say the *s*-word?!"

"Mommy knows you're not stupid," my mom said. "But for safety, you need to let me or Daddy unbuckle you."

That didn't make any sense to me, but before I could tell her that, a woman's voice called out. "Oh, are you the neighbours?"

My mom's face was tense, but she looked up anyway. "I... yes. This is our house."

A woman with blue eyes, white skin and dark brown hair that matched the little girl's smiled at my mom from the walkway. She was holding a baby and wearing a blue dress.

"I am so sorry we blocked the driveway," she said. "The movers needed to lower the ramp so they could get some of the heavier items out."

A man with blonde hair came up behind her. "Do you need them to move?"

"Oh, not at all," my mom said. "We can park on the street for now."

It was clearly a boring grown-up conversation, so I turned back to the little girl.

"So can I keep playing here?" she asked. "If I give you braids?"

"Well, okay," I said, dropping to the ground beside her. "But they better be pretty braids."

"I said you'd get braids, not that they'd be pretty," she said. "If you want them to be pretty, you have to be my best friend."

"What if I don't want to be your best friend?"

She shrugged. "I'll tangle your hair up in the sticks and your mom'll have to cut it off."

Vaguely threatening as it was, it made perfect sense to me. "Okay. We can be best friends."

She perked up and whirled the upper half of her body around.

"Mommy!" she screeched. "I don't hate it here anymore! I made a best friend."

"That's excellent, *chérie*," said the woman before turning to talk to my mom again.

"What's your name?" I asked when the girl turned back to me.

"Anne-Marie," she said. "What's yours?"

"Nellie."

She nodded with an almost business-like preciseness. "Are you ready to be beautiful, Nellie?"

"I was born ready," I said.

Not that I knew what it meant, but my mom said it earlier and it sounded cool.

At some point, my dad walked by to join my mom in talking to the new neighbours. I wasn't paying attention because Anne-Marie told me her hair toy would tear my hair out if I moved too much. The two of us sat there, playing in the grass and learning all the things we deemed important to know about best friends, like our favourite animals and favourite dinosaurs and which of us had been caught in quicksand more times.

I didn't know what quicksand actually was, but Anne-Marie said her brother had been caught in it once and I said that didn't count because he wasn't there.

"Okay, but have you ever rode a horse?" Anne-Marie asked.

"No," I said.

She smiled as if she'd won something. "I have. Like every day, almost, when we lived in Toronto. It's why I said I was going to hate it here."

I pretended I wasn't jealous. "Yeah, well, I rode a dolphin once."

"No you didn't."

"Yes, I did."

"How?" She folded her arms. "Dolphins don't live in Montreal."

Before I could respond, an older boy with floppy blonde hair and a gap in the teeth on the left side of his mouth skipped across the driveway.

"Anne-Marie," he said in a bossy voice. "Mom said you have to tell the movers where you want to put your Barbie Dream House."

I instantly forgot I was trying to one-up Anne-Marie on everything. "You have a Barbie Dream House?!"

Anne-Marie nodded. "Yeah. Wanna come see?"

"Yeah!"

We both scrambled to our feet, but before I could move, the older boy stepped in front of us and folded his arms.

"No strangers in the house," he said.

"I'm not a stranger," I said. "I'm Nellie."

"Well, I've never heard of you," he said. "So you're a stranger and you can't come in."

"Stop being stupid, Jean-Paul," Anne-Marie said. "Nellie is my best friend and she's allowed in the house because I said so."

"You can't say the s-word!" he scolded.

"Why are you so bossy?" I asked.

"Because I'm nine and you have to listen to me," he said, then looked back at his sister. "And I *said* I want to be called JP."

She shrugged. "Then be nice to me and my new best friend."

He huffed. "Fine. But I'm coming with you to make sure she doesn't wreck anything."

"She won't," Anne-Marie said, grabbing my hand.

There were three stone steps that lead to a small landing at the front door, but before we reached the first one, I let go of Anne-Marie's hand and whirled around, putting my hands on my hips. JP stumbled, catching himself just before he crashed into me.

"What are you doing?!" he demanded.

"You can't come in," I said.

"I can, too," he said.

"Nope. You're a stranger. So if no strangers are allowed in the house, you can't go in."

"I'm not a stranger!" he insisted. "*You're* a stranger! And it's not your house!"

"Mo-*om*!" I hollered. "A stranger is trying to get into the neighbour's house!"

JP's mouth dropped open. He let out a loud, disbelieving scoff, then turned to where our parents were standing.

"Nellie, I think he lives there," my mom said.

"I dunno," Anne-Marie said. "I've never seen him before in my life."

"See?" I said. "Also he smells bad."

"Hey!" JP said, glaring at me.

"Kids," said the blonde man, who must have been Anne-Marie's dad.

"Anne-Marie, be nice to your brother," said Anne-Marie's mom.

"I am very nice to Marc-Andre," Anne-Marie said, motioning to the baby her mom was holding.

"You need to be nice to *both* of your brothers. And, uh…?" She trailed off, looking at me.

"Nellie," my dad said.

"Nellie," she continued. "Thank you so much for watching out for our house, but Jean-Paul is allowed inside. He lives there."

"It's JP, Mom," JP grumbled.

"What if he's an imposter?" I said.

"I'm *not!*" JP said.

"You smell like one," Anne-Marie said.

"And no one likes a Bossy Bessie," I said, which was what my mom said when I was being bossy.

He glared at me. "Just move, Nellie. My mom said you have to."

I kept my hands on my hips. "She said you were allowed inside. Not that I have to move."

JP stared at me. I stared back, chin jutting out partially from stubbornness and partially because he was a big kid and I was a little kid so I had to look up at him. He drew in a breath and for a moment, I thought he was going to turn around and tattle on me to our parents.

Instead, I let out a yelp of surprise as he stepped forward, picked me up by the waist, and turned to the right before setting me down in the flower bed beside the door. It happened so fast that I barely reacted, staring at him with wide eyes until I felt myself sinking and looked down.

"Oh *no!*" I said in horror.

"Ohmigod," Anne-Marie whimpered. "Is it quicksand?"

"I—" I tried to lift my leg, but I couldn't. "I-I'm *stuck!*" My neck snapped back up to JP. "Help me out."

"Mmm... nah," he said.

And that was when I hollered that I was done with men and my mom rushed across the driveway to help me while my dad looked perturbed at the mess my shoes were leaving on the sidewalk.

"Really, do not worry about it," Anne-Marie's mom was saying to him. "Jean-Paul can sweep it up when it dries."

"Why do I have to clean it up?" JP asked indignantly.

"Because it's your fault!" Anne-Marie said, her voice ringing with—in my opinion—righteous indigence. "You put her there!"

"I didn't know the dirt was wet, stupid."

"Mom!" Anne-Marie screeched.

"Jean-Paul," the woman scolded. "Don't call your sister the s-word!"

He huffed, folding his arms. "I *said* my name is JP!"

"And it stands for Jerk Pants," I said.

"It does not," snapped JP.

"Maybe you shouldn't be such a jerk pants, then."

My mom, who was crouched down and attempting to wipe some of the chunks of mud off my shoes, looked at me. Her eyes were crinkling like they did when she laughed, but she was shaking her head. "Nellie, you can't call the new neighbour Jerk Pants. Be nice."

"I don't *want* to be nice!" Stinging tears welled up in my eyes and I clenched my fists. "He's not nice! He's mean and bossy and he wrecked my new *shoes*!"

She said something that was meant to calm me down, but it was too late. A too big, too intense, too overwhelming feeling took over and I started sobbing. My mom put a hand on my arm but I thrashed away from her.

"Nellie, stop," she said, and that time she tried to grab me with both hands.

So naturally, since *someone* had just done the same thing and caused this whole mess in the first place, I tried to escape her grasp.

But because JP Marchand was a gigantic stupid jerk pants, my gorgeous light-up sneakers were covered in thick, chunky, and—worst of all—*sticky* mud.

So instead of escaping, I lost my balance and tumbled to the ground.

In the moments between landing on my butt beside the twin holes my feet had left in the muddy flower bed and throwing what my dad eventually referred to as the single most horrifically embarrassing temper tantrum he'd ever had the misfortune of witnessing, I looked up. JP was looking back at me, his lips curled down and his eyes sparkling as he tried not to laugh.

And maybe I didn't know what it meant to be done with men, like I'd screeched earlier.

But I decided right then and there that I was absolutely, positively, one-hundred-percent *done* with JP Marchand.

Chapter One
The Five Stages of Fucking Up

I'D NEVER BEEN QUITE so proud of myself as I was when Adrian started crying.

He'd gone through the first three stages of grief relatively quickly. At least, he had once he'd processed what I said. Because at first, he sat on the couch, staring up at me like the hamster in his brain had overslept and was stumbling around frantically, spilling coffee from a hamster-sized cup as it scurried about in its socks, trying to find its briefcase and keys before saying fuck it and clamouring into the wheel to start turning it.

That was when Adrian blinked and went into denial.

"You're not breaking up with me," he said.

"Yes, I am," I replied.

He blinked at me twice more, then frowned.

"You can't fucking do that," he'd said.

Anger.

"I just did," I said.

He let out an incredulous scoff, glancing to the side as if to regroup before looking back at me.

"Give me a chance here," he said. "Let's talk about this first."

Bargaining, right on time and what I'd been waiting for.

"What is there to talk about?" I asked.

"Whatever happened to cause this," he said. "We have something special, Nellie. At least, I thought we did."

"So did I," I said, unfolding my arms so I could open my messenger bag and dig out the brand-new laptop my dad had gotten me for my birthday the previous week. "But apparently what we *had* isn't enough for you. Or at least, it's not special enough to keep you from saying the most heinous shit I've ever seen in my life."

He had the audacity to look confused. "What do you—"

"'Nah, just me and my hand,'" I read from the screen, keeping the laptop propped up on my forearm as I balanced it with my other hand. "'She's at some fucking volleyball tournament again.'" I changed my voice to an approximation of what I thought the other person might sound like. "'Thought she wasn't putting out anyway?'"

Adrian's face turned a ghastly shade of greyish-white. His mouth was still half-open, but nothing came out. "Wait—"

"'Yeah, but someone else's hand is always nice. Or maybe if I beg enough she'll use her mouth,'" I continued. "'I'm desperate to get my dick wet, though. But she's such a fucking prude. We've been together since she was in tenth grade. Two years and she still won't put out.'"

"Wait," he said. "Just let me—"

"'You're more patient than I would be. I'd be doing a hell of a lot more to get my way, if you know what I mean.'" I switched my voice back to normal. "'Yeah, well, maybe I should'"—I paused, looking directly at Adrian and then enunciating the next five words so clearly that he winced—"'*accidentally let it slip in* next time we're fooling around so she realizes it's not the big deal she thinks it is.'"

"No," he said. "I would *never*—"

"'LOL,'" I read. "'Yeah, like, sorry baby, I tripped and fell, but if it's in there anyway...'"

"It's guy talk," he said desperately.

"Guys talk about tricking people into having sex by 'accidentally' slipping it in?" I asked, raising my eyebrows. "Pretty sure there's a word for people who force their girlfriends to have sex, Adrian. Is that what you are?"

And that was when he started crying.

Depression.

Right on time.

I'd hoped I'd make him cry. I'd hoped I wasn't *so* wrong about Adrian that he wouldn't have any remorse for what he'd said. Or at least, I'd hoped that there was enough of the boy I'd originally fallen for left in him to feel bad about it.

Because back when I was in tenth grade and he was in eleventh, this wasn't who he was. Not even a little. He'd been funny and romantic and loving. There were days when we'd start a video call after dinner and wouldn't hang up until we saw each other on the walk to school the next morning. Some nights, we'd start watching a movie at the same time and make comments here and there, and we'd both eventually fall asleep with our phones next to our heads.

But we would also talk, sometimes until a few hours before we had to wake up for school. Whispered conversations where we'd share vulnerable things, those feelings and fears and hopes that were so brand new to us. We'd talk about everything from our childhoods to the anxiety we were both feeling about him going to university while I was still in high school.

And we'd talk about sex.

"I don't know if I'm ready," he'd said one night. "I want to, but it feels…"

"Too soon?" I asked, trying not to sound disappointed. "We've been together for a long time."

"I know," he said. "But it's like there are no—"

"Like there are no take-backs," I finished. "I know. We can wait until we're ready."

I didn't say that I was ready and had been for months. I was sure Adrian knew I was ready because I'd mentioned it vaguely a couple of times, but I wasn't ready for him to know *how* ready I was.

It was a little embarrassing. Like, I knew teenage hormones were a thing, but everyone always said that guys had it worse when it came to the... you know. *Horniness* aspect. I didn't want Adrian to think I was weird for how much I wanted to try having sex.

But God, did I want to.

"You know I want it to be you," Adrian said, the glow from the phone screen flickering as he adjusted his blankets.

"I want it to be you, too," I said.

"Never wanted anyone but you."

"Me neither."

Both of us were trying to hide our smiles beneath our blankets as we talked like we were old enough to have ever considered having sex with anyone else instead of recognizing that we were high school sweethearts who started talking about sex barely a year earlier.

"There's no rush," I said. "We can keep doing what we're doing until we both feel ready."

"I do like what we're doing," he murmured. "A *lot*."

I grinned, laughing into my blankets so the sound was muffled. Of course he liked what we were doing. He got to play with my boobs and up until a couple of months earlier, sit back and relax while I gave him a handjob.

Then I'd forgotten his birthday over the summer.

It wasn't my fault. I mean, it was, because I was the one who forgot, but it was because I was babysitting full-time for a little boy named Bodhi and we'd gone to Canada's Wonderland that day. I'd been a little distracted by all the rides and when I got home, Adrian had called and said he'd be at my mom's place in ten minutes to pick me up for dinner. So with no time to get a last-minute gift and scrambling to cover the fact that I hadn't gotten him a gift, I impulsively offered him a blowjob for the first time.

Of course he liked that.

I didn't mind it all that much either. Unlike when I gave him a handjob, a blowjob didn't last all that long. It didn't taste as bad as I thought it would, so we'd been doing a lot more of *that* since then because the faster he came, the faster I would get my turn. And he was getting a lot better with his fingers. The last couple of times we'd messed around, I'd almost finished without having to do it myself.

That was as far as we'd gone. Which wasn't a problem.

But then he'd started university.

"Nellie, I swear I wouldn't," Adrian sobbed as I stood in front of him with those horrible messages displayed on my laptop screen. "I was trying to fit in with the guys and—"

"You were the one who wanted to wait!"

"I know." He put his elbows on his knees, burying his face in his hands as he cried. "I know. I'm sorry. Look, I know I don't deserve you, but I would never—I *will* never—"

"Exactly," I interrupted, closing my laptop. "You will *never* have sex with me. Because we're breaking up."

Another sob racked him as he looked up. "Nellie, please."

I put the laptop back in my bag. "You know, if you'd asked, I would've had sex with you. I've wanted to for ages."

His eyes went wide. "What? But—"

"You always said you weren't ready." I shrugged. "I was trying to be supportive and not pressure you. But you know what the silver lining of us breaking up is? Now I can go find someone else who'll respect me more to have that experience with. And you can find someone who's less of a 'prude' to 'get your dick wet' with." I turned to leave, then stopped.

"Oh, and before you complain to all your new friends about how your ex-girlfriend is a total psycho who spied on you or something? Make sure you log out of someone's laptop after you use it to complain about them."

"I won't—"

"And also, I didn't say you could use my laptop when you came over. The overall lesson for you here is just fucking *ask*, Adrian, okay?"

And then I left.

If I'd been smart, I wouldn't have. But since he'd gone so smoothly through the other stages of grief, I thought acceptance would be easy for him, too.

But the thing is, I'd assumed the stages of grief applied here when really, Adrian was faced with the five stages of someone finding out you fucked up *real* bad. And those stages are different because some people, when faced with self-imposed misery, do not accept it.

They enter the fifth stage of fucking up, which is damage control.

Chapter Two
A Deal With The Devil

FOUR MONTHS TO THE day after I'd broken up with Adrian was the worst best day of my life.

"Oh, Daughter of Mine," my mom called in a sing-song voice as I walked in the house after school, dragging my feet as I tried to figure out how to explain the letter in my backpack.

"Hey, Mom," I said. "What's up?"

She bounded out of the kitchen and into the entryway, still wearing the collared blue LCBO shirt and dress pants that were the uniform of the liquor store she managed, her blonde hair pulled back in two long Dutch braids. In her hand was a torn-open envelope.

The Drop Tower ride at Canada's Wonderland fell slower than my heart did at that moment. My eyes laser-focused on the envelope and my mind got caught in a whirlwind of wondering why they would've sent her a letter directly and *how* she'd gotten it and why she was *smiling*, of all things.

"I... I can explain," I said.

"Explain *what*?!" she asked. "Lord thunderin' Jesus, you want me to explain that my daughter is a right genius and I'm about t'dance naked down the streets and shout it so everyone between here and the Detention Center knows it?"

That seemed like an odd response, especially since her Newfoundland accent was slipping into her voice. Which only happened when she was excited, angry, or incredibly drunk. And anger would have made sense, but not with what she was saying. "What?"

She waved the envelope in the air and started talking so fast that I almost couldn't keep up. "Don't be mad, ducky. I wasn't minding the names when I was opening the mail and I wasn't expectin' ya to be geddin a letter, 'specially not one so damn proper." She held up the envelope, but I didn't catch what the printed logo was before she flipped it over and tugged the letter back out. "So wasn't till I read it that—oh, well, *look*!"

She shoved the letter at me and I took it, glancing down.

Dear Ms. Belanger,

We are pleased to offer you admission to the Ottawa Institute of Technology and acceptance into the BSc Forensic Science program—

I burst into tears.

"Oh, my girl," Mom said, throwing her arms around me. "You did it. You *did* it!"

For a few minutes, all I could do was cry. Mom held onto me the whole time, rocking back and forth in celebration. She probably thought I was crying from happiness, and I mean, I *was*. Most of the tears were good ones; tears of relief and pride and excitement.

But some of them were tears I'd bottled up throughout the day that slipped out alongside the happy ones.

"We're celebrating tonight," Mom declared when I regained control of my emotions. She let go of me and took the letter from me, smoothing out a wrinkle on the edge where I'd been clutching it. "I'll order from Thai Kitchen and pop by work when I go to pick it up." She bumped me with her hip. "This way we can have champagne."

My face brightened. I was eighteen, but the drinking age in Ontario was nineteen. "Really?"

"Best kind. Good news calls for good bubbles. 'Less you want something else, Miss University Student. Nothin' hard, though. Not on a school night."

"Um... well." My excitement faded and I squirmed away from her arm so I could get to my backpack. "Funnily enough, I need you to sign something for me."

Mom's smile faded as I pulled a folded letter out of my bag. "What do you mean, *sign* something for you?"

I didn't respond. I didn't even look at her. I just handed her the paper and tried not to shake as I felt her eyes on me for a long, terrifying moment before she looked at it. The silence was so quiet that I could almost hear my mom's eyes moving back and forth as she read. Finally, after a long moment, she sighed, and all the Newfoundland was gone from her voice.

Which meant she wasn't "right rotted."

She wasn't mad.

She was disappointed.

"Nellie," she said.

"I can explain," I said.

She folded the letter, then changed her mind and re-opened it. "You had better start explaining then, missy."

"Ms. Ellerby was talking shit about me."

"Ms. Ellerby... the English teacher for the English class you nearly failed?"

"*Yes,*" I said. "She has it out for me and—"

"Considering you were flunking English long before Ms. Ellerby got involved, you understand it very much sounds like you're making up an excuse for calling her a"—she referenced the letter again—"'a lying thundercunt who wants to be one of the popular girls because she was too ugly to be a skank in high school'?"

"Wow. They actually wrote that out?" I said.

"I'm assuming the asterisk between the 'C' and the 'N' is meant to be a 'U' and unless you called her a skunk, the other asterisk is an 'A.'"

"Skunk would've been funny too," I muttered.

"Nellie!"

"Mom, she—"

"You cannot call your teachers *cunts*!" she snapped. "You shouldn't be calling *anyone* a cunt, but goddamn."

"So skank is okay, then?"

She glared at me, which was fair.

"Mom, I swear. I *heard* her say something about me," I said. "She didn't know I was in the library because Courtney and all her dickhead friends were surrounding her asking if the health assembly that they cancelled classes for tomorrow was because *someone* couldn't keep her legs closed and—"

I stopped talking. Mom gave me an unimpressed look, but when she realized I'd gone silent because I was about to cry again, her expression changed. I didn't know if she believed me, but at the very least, she'd softened enough to listen.

"Hon, you don't know that they meant you," she said.

"Ms. Ellerby told them to thank me for being able to take the period off and they all laughed."

"She specifically said your name?"

"Well, no, but—" "

"*Nellie*—"

"—she said 'Loose Nell.'"

I think my mom's face invented a new shade of red. "She called you *what*?"

"I know they all call me that, but she's a teacher, so it was just—"

"—fucking unacceptable," she spat.

"But Mr. McSheffrey didn't believe me." I gestured at the letter. "He said that they do the sexual health assembly every year and it's been planned for months, so it has nothing to do with me and Ms. Ellerby would know that. And the only people in the library were Courtney and her friends. Everyone else was at lunch. So no one else heard what happened."

Mom's lip puffed out and I knew she was running her tongue along her teeth as she studied the letter.

"So you got suspended," she said. "In-school for the rest of the day and at-home until the end of the week. And you have to write an apology letter to Ms. Ellerby."

"I already wrote the letter," I said. "But you have to sign it as proof I told you about it."

She rolled her eyes. "You're eighteen. You're an adult. Sign it yourself."

"I told them that, but Mr. McSheffrey said that's not the point."

She held her hand out. I dug into my bag and took out my notebook and a pen, finding the page I'd written the letter on and tearing it away from the spirals. Mom took it and read it in silence.

"It would make things worse if I wrote 'I acknowledge Nellie's error and will discuss with her how to appropriately react when she has a lying thundercunt for an English teacher' with my signature, wouldn't it?" she asked.

"Probably."

She sighed. "I thought so."

"I'm not saying you shouldn't."

She chuckled, then scribbled her signature on the bottom of the notebook paper and the letter the principal had sent home.

"Out of school suspension isn't a vacation," she said after handing it back to me. "You're going to tidy the house. Clean the bathrooms, reorganize the pantry, go through that pile of junk in the crawlspace and those boxes you have in your closet of random crap you don't know what to do with since you'll have to go through it anyway when you leave for university."

"I still have to do my schoolwork," I said.

"We both know you've got it done," she said. "You're taking classes you like this semester. Which means you're applying yourself and being the genius I know you are instead of someone who can't pay attention in English class."

"I don't like reading," I said in exasperation. "It's boring and—"

"Not the point. What I'm saying is that if you haven't already done the work you need to for the next three days on your own time because you felt like it, you finished it all during your in-school suspension."

I glanced down, running my fingernail along the edge of my thumb as anger prickled up my spine. She wasn't *technically* right, but that was only because my calculus prof hadn't mailed me the worksheets I needed yet.

But the whole thing was getting worse and worse.

The only thing I hated more than apologizing—*especially* when I wasn't in the wrong, and frankly, I'd been nicer to Ms. Ellerby than she'd deserved—was cleaning. Which my mom knew because she was the exact same way.

She knew just how much it would suck to go through all the boxes and bags in my closet, trying to figure out what to do with things I'd shoved in there at the end of other cleaning sessions because I didn't know what else to do with them. Things that weren't garbage but that I couldn't give away; cords for electronic devices I might never need and mementos from random events and old journals from when my parents divorced that I couldn't bring myself to throw out even though whenever I opened those boxes, I couldn't stop myself from flipping through them and remembering how painful that period had been.

I don't know why I did it. Most of the time, I wanted to forget the way Mom told me we were moving to Toronto or the quiet look of satisfaction on my dad's face as I cried that I didn't want to go. I didn't want to think about how the house I'd grown up in had always seemed big, but became cavernous once the warmth and love was sheared in two by a set of divorce papers. I wanted to forget the way I procrastinated packing up my room as my dad made offer after offer to my mom, trying to get her to reconsider taking me away from Montreal, because I wanted her to accept one of them.

I wanted to forget the hurt in her voice when she came into my room and realized I hadn't started packing.

I wanted to forget the way my dad stood outside that big, nearly empty house as my mom backed down the driveway, the neutral and businesslike look on his face so practiced from years of boardroom meetings and networking with colleagues that it seemed almost natural, and so contrary to the way he'd pleaded with my mom to stay in Montreal.

And I really, really wanted to forget that as she cranked the steering wheel to turn onto the street, I could've sworn that from the corner of my eye, I saw my dad wipe a tear off his face.

But by the time I looked more closely, he'd turned around and was walking towards the front door.

As much as I wanted to forget, whenever I saw those journals with some pages torn out and others with gouges in them from something being scribbled out aggressively on the previous page and some of them with dried teardrops blurring the shaky eleven-year-old printing, I opened them and relived it all.

My mom didn't know that, of course. She would've never punished me with something like that. If she'd known, she would've gone into those boxes herself, grabbed the journals, and thrown them in the

Toronto Harbour while I was at school so I never had to think about that time again. And maybe I should've told her about them.

But maybe I was making my punishment about more than chores on purpose.

I started on some of the chores while Mom took a shower and then left to pick up dinner. Which meant by the time she returned with an order of pad thai for me and tom yum soup for her, I was still cranky and upset, but she was as bubbly as the bottle of champagne she'd bought.

"Let's figure out a plan for next year," she said. "We'll do up a budget for your tuition and books and look at rentals in Ottawa to get an idea of how much it'll cost and—"

"There's still lots of time before I have to do any of that," I said. "I just got accepted today."

But my mom was the kind of person who got excited and wanted to do everything all at once. And I didn't want to push any more buttons lest she add more to her list of chores. So instead of doing what I wanted after dinner, which was go to my room and stare blankly at the string lights on the ceiling while trying to process the day, I brought my laptop to the kitchen table.

And that was when everything got even worse.

"—which means you..." Mom trailed off as she stared at the screen.

"I don't have enough," I said.

She twisted her mouth to the side, bouncing her leg as she studied the spreadsheet.

"I mean, it's not a big deal," I said. "I'll ask Dad—"

"No."

The word was like ice cracking, loud and sudden and sharp. I froze in place, then twisted to look at her, confusion on my face. "What?"

"You are not asking him for money."

That cleared up absolutely nothing. "But I'm sure he'll pay for—"

"Oh, he will," she said. "He'll pay for everything. But you know what happens when you make a deal with the devil, Nellie?"

I picked at the skin on my thumb again, uncomfortable as I looked back at the laptop. My mom had a lot of names she called my dad, including a number of variations that implied he was literally Satan.

"The devil collects," she said when I didn't answer.

"I thought he was supposed to contribute to my education," I said. "Like, didn't the court say—"

"'Supposed to contribute' is very different from 'Something you should accept,'" she interrupted. "Nellie, you got a gift when you turned eighteen. You don't ever have to see that man again. Don't throw that gift away for this."

"For this?" I repeated. "You mean for my education? For my *career*?"

"Trust me, Daughter of Mine." She shook her head. "You've got scholarships, too. Together, it almost covers the tuition."

"Almost isn't fully," I said. "And I'll need money for books. And food. And rent. And three more years of school after this."

"Student loans are an option."

"You'd rather me go into debt than ask Dad?"

Her thumbnail ended up in her mouth and she chewed on it, staring at the computer screen.

"What if you... didn't go to Ottawa?" she asked.

I stared at her until she looked up.

"You haven't heard back from the University of Toronto yet," she said. "You'd save a lot of money if you went there and—"

"I don't want to go to U of T!"

"Why?"

I sputtered for a moment. "Because Ottawa Tech was my first choice!"

"Yes, but U of T was always on your list. What changed?"

"Ottawa Tech has the best forensic science program in—"

"The real reason," she said.

My heart was racing almost painfully. "That *is* the real reason!"

"Are you sure?"

"What else would it be?"

"I think we both know." She folded her arms. "You need to do what's best for you, Nellie. Just because Adrian goes to U of T doesn't mean you shouldn't. You can't let what he said control your life."

Mom and I didn't fight often, but when we did, it was explosive.

And that one... I mean, it was a wonder the neighbours didn't call the bomb squad.

Because I'd *never* felt anger like that.

I'd never cried like that.

I'd never felt so betrayed by my own mother.

"Nellie, I'm *sorry*!" she finally shouted after we'd been fighting long enough that my throat was dry and raw, partially from the yelling and partially because it felt like every drop of moisture in my body had spilled out of my eyes and down my cheeks. "I know it's been hard dealing with the fallout of the rumours the past few months, but—"

"Fuck off," I sobbed, pushing my chair back and snatching my laptop off the table, along with the acceptance letter and the scraps of paper we'd been using to brainstorm all the things I'd need for school. "Fuck *all* the way off. How *dare* you think I'd do this because of him? Just because *you* uprooted your whole life and decided to live with nothing to get away from your husband doesn't mean *I* would do the same!"

She reacted as though my words had physically stung her. Which I'd meant them to, but I still felt bad about it, even as the outline of her face blurred with the fresh tears pooling in my eyes.

"I want better for you," she said.

"Then why are you stopping me from doing the best thing for me?"

"Honey—"

"I'm done." I shoved the back of my hand across my face, nearly giving myself a paper cut on my forehead with the acceptance letter. "I'm going to bed."

"It's seven-thirty."

"Good night."

She didn't come in to check on me after I slammed my bedroom door. Not because she didn't care; both of us knew when I needed space, I needed *space*. I needed my bed and a pillow to scream-cry into and no witnesses to see how red my face got when I was sobbing so hard that I couldn't breathe.

And God, did I need all of that right then.

But she should have checked on me.

She really, really should have.

I wasn't lying when I said if U of T had the program I wanted to do, I would go there regardless. Like sure, maybe if it *actually* did, I would've changed that opinion. I couldn't deny that while U of T might have a big campus, it felt like the whole of Toronto wasn't big enough to get away from the things Adrian had said and done. But hypothetically, I would've done the right thing.

I would've done what was best for me.

Argument or not, that was one thing my mom was right about.

We just disagreed about what we thought was best for me. Which is why she should checked on me.

Because maybe if she had, she would've got her way.

Chapter Three
Ma Fille Ange

"*Ma fille ange!*"

I almost fell over as the man I would've considered the textbook definition of composure hugged me.

I mean, he didn't hug me hard. But the hug in general was a shock.

"Hi, Dad," I said, my voice muffled by the shoulder of his suit jacket as I hugged him back.

He let go, stepping back but keeping a hand on my shoulder as he looked me over. "Did you have a safe drive? I know it is a long trip from Toronto, but you seem to have made excellent time."

"I did," I said. "Traffic wasn't nearly as bad as I thought it would be for the long weekend."

"Ah, well. Most people would have left for their cottages yesterday, I suppose." He glanced down at the backpack I'd set on the floor beside me. "You have more of your things in your car, yes?"

I nodded. "I figured I'd come in and say hi before I started unloading—"

"Nonsense. I will have Pierre unload the car and bring your things to your room. Leave your keys on the table." He motioned to an expensive-looking solid wood table next to the door that contained a single decorative bowl. "In the meantime, I would like you to meet someone."

I wasn't entirely sure how he did it, but my dad had a way of smiling that kept the corners of his eyes from folding into those happy little crinkles that most people got. At least, mostly. Faint lines had started to appear around the edges of his greyish-blue eyes, though still not enough of them to quash the surprise most people had when they found out he was in his fifties. Like every other expression he made, it was a controlled look, and I'd seen it enough times throughout my teen years to know exactly what kind of person he would like me to meet without even having to look behind him to see the tall, thin, platinum blonde woman with a glowing golden spray tan entering the foyer.

"Nellie, *ange*, I would like you to meet my girlfriend," my dad said in a smooth, deliberate voice. "This is Brayleigh."

She couldn't have been much older than me, but I smiled all the same. "It's nice to meet you."

"I'm *so* excited to meet you," Brayleigh said in a voice that sounded like the auditory equivalent of icing oozing from a piping bag. "It's so nice of your mom to finally let you come and spend some time with Max."

She must have been a really new girlfriend to mention my mom casually like that. The smile on my dad's lips tightened into one that wasn't a smile at all.

"Yes," he said, his voice cold at the reminder of the one woman he couldn't keep, even with all his money. "After all that has happened, I am spoiled to spend a whole summer with my beautiful daughter." He looked at me, then shook his head. "You grow up so much each time I see you. University already? Was it not just yesterday that you were sitting on the rug in my office practicing your multiplication tables?"

"Maybe not yesterday, but I think I did some math homework last time I visited," I said. "That could be what you're thinking of?"

He laughed. "Clever girl. But perhaps, considering that was… well. Thanksgiving, was it not?"

Tension threaded in his voice again, a hint of his annoyance that I hadn't visited for nearly eight months—before Adrian and I had even broken up.

"Yeah," I said, trying to look forlorn. "I wish something would have worked out, but between diplomas and grad and stuff…"

"Hmm," he said. No smile, but he seemed to accept what I'd said and clapped his hands together. "Well, the past is the past. I am not quite finished with my work day yet. I need only a few more hours, so perhaps you can spend some time getting to know Brayleigh while you settle in. Then the three of us will go for dinner. Beaujolais Park, perhaps?"

"Sure," I said.

"That sounds wonderful," Brayleigh said. "Shall I call to make a reservation?"

My dad nodded, then pulled me in for another hug and kissed the side of my head. "*Merci, ma fille ange*. I am so glad you are here."

He walked away, his shoes clicking on the floor as he headed to his office at the back of the house. Brayleigh and I both watched him go, then I turned to her.

"So—" I started.

"Stay out of my way and I'll stay out of yours."

Her demeanour went from champagne bubbles to barracuda before I even blinked. I stared at her, stunned at the sudden shift. "What makes you think I want to get in your way?"

A bubblegum pink lip curled up into a sneer and she pointed one long, talon-like nail at me. "Spoiled little princesses like you always do, little *'angel girl.'* And I have spent far too much time with your father to let some snotty child ruin that."

I laughed. I had to. The swell of incredulous disbelief had to come out somehow. "If I'm a child, what does that make you?"

"Excuse me?"

"I'm eighteen," I said, then looked her up and down. "He's fifty-two and you're what, thirty?"

She looked *horrified*. "How dare you? I am twenty-five."

"Huh," I said, then shrugged. "I guess I should've figured that out. I don't think he's been with anyone in her thirties since my mom. Either way, you aren't old enough to pass for my mother, so if I'm a child, you're a teenager at best."

"You're a snotty brat is what you are," she said, and I was almost surprised I could tell her face was turning red though the fake tan on her white skin. "Just don't fuck with me, understand, Eleanor?"

"It's Nellie."

She ignored me, turning on a heel and clacking away down the hall, leaving me standing in the foyer of my dad's gigantic house by myself. I watched as she turned the corner, then let out a shaky breath.

God*damn.*

My dad had introduced me to plenty of girlfriends over the years. I wasn't so naïve to think they all liked me, but none of them had outright stated it the way Brayleigh had. I usually saw the same one about three times before they broke up. The woman he'd been with when I last visited had been the record holder—a significant six visits, including the couple of weeks I spent with him over the summer.

My dad's girlfriends always fell into one of two camps. They were either tall, blonde, and dead set on getting on my good side so I'd be an ally in their quest to be the next Mrs. Maximillian Belanger—colloquially only, of course, since women couldn't take their husbands' last names in Quebec—or tall, blonde, and certain that I was going to be detrimental to their plans to become the next Mrs. Maximillian Belanger.

Both strategies were stupid, of course. Dad wasn't with women who were a couple of decades younger than him because he was going to marry them.

Well, except my mom.

Although, he hadn't intended to marry her, either.

But she'd been different. I was pretty sure my dad had been different, too. There was no way to prove it, of course, but seeing as my mom considered him to be the worst thing in her life and my dad—shrewd and clever though he could be when it came to business and finance and the stock market—was a dumbass who couldn't see that he was trying to replace my mom with his progressively younger models of blondes, I had a feeling I was right.

They had never made sense together. My mom was a free spirit who loved dancing and sailing and animals, while my dad was a hedge fund manager who worked constantly and put far more importance on appearances than he should. But somehow, those two very smart people were idiots in love and when my mom peed on a stick and realized the spontaneous Valentine's Day fling she'd had with some guy at a business convention she'd been waitressing at had resulted in yours truly, my dad decided to marry her.

Somehow, it took eleven years for them to realize they were at opposite ends of the personality spectrum. When my mom couldn't take it anymore, she left, and my dad, too stubborn to admit he'd lost the best thing that had ever happened to him, began working his way through the long line of potential successors to her position with little to no success while my mom just... worked.

Hard.

I didn't understand it. I mean, it wasn't like I thought my mom should stay in a marriage where she was unhappy. But my mom wasn't known for being particularly discreet and I was a snoopy kid who eavesdropped a lot, so I knew my dad had offered her way more in the divorce than she'd taken. Alimony she wasn't entitled to because she'd signed a pre-nup. Child support payments far above what the courts agreed he should pay. A house—he'd offered to buy her a fucking house in Montreal.

And she'd said no to it all.

I didn't know why, but she was adamant that she get the bare minimum financially so that he, in turn, would get the bare minimum when it came to custody. She walked away with nothing more than the federally-mandated amount of child support and my dad got custody for one weekend a month—a long weekend whenever possible because of travel time from Toronto—the majority of spring break, alternating major holidays, and two weeks during the summer. And my mom worked her ass off, doing everything she could so that she could take care of both of us while using as little of the money my dad sent for child support as she could so she could save that for me to go to university.

Which had been pretty idealistic of her, considering where I was now.

I mean, I hated to lie to her. I *hated* it. But after that explosive fight when she thought I was refusing to go to U of T because of *Adrian*, I didn't have a choice.

I'd tried. There were still tears on my face when I opened my laptop and went to the website to see how much of a student loan I'd qualify for. But considering how high my dad's income was, I was surprised the website I'd plugged my information into didn't respond with just a gif of someone falling off a chair because they were laughing so hard.

I didn't need to do the math, but I did anyway. Working over the summer wouldn't earn me enough. A part-time job would barely make a dent in what I needed.

So that same night, I'd put a pile of dirty laundry on top of my vent and crammed pillows against the crack under my door so my voice wouldn't travel through the house—something I'd learned from all those late-night video chats with Adrian. Then I'd gotten into bed and buried myself beneath the blankets to muffle the sound even further.

He answered on the third ring. "*Oui?*"

"Dad?"

He paused. When he spoke again, there was no surprise in his voice, as though a phone call from me was a weekly occurrence instead of something that hadn't happened for months. "Yes, Eleanor?"

"It's... it's still Nellie," I said. "Hi."

"Is something wrong?"

Yeah, of course there was something wrong, but I forced a laugh. "Not at all. I, um, wanted to share some good news with you."

"Good news," he repeated. "Well, you know I always want to hear good news from my beautiful daughter."

"Yeah." I forced another laugh. "I, um, got into Ottawa Tech."

"Well, that is magnificent," he said, his tone pleasant but still controlled. "Congratulations. You are pleased, obviously. What will you be taking?"

"I got into the Forensic Science program. It's, um, the best one in the country."

"Ah. And that will lead to a... *gainful* sort of career?"

"I mean, yeah. I want to be a forensic scientist, so..."

"Could that be beneficial for acceptance into law school?" he asked. "I have always thought you would make an excellent lawyer."

My dad had always dreamed I'd go to law school, but I had absolutely no desire to be a lawyer. But reminding him of that didn't seem especially helpful just then. "I mean, yeah. It could definitely be useful if that's what I wanted to do."

"Ah," he said again, though his tone was more impressed. "Well, I do hope you consider it, Nellie. When do you begin classes?"

I picked at the skin around my thumb. "Well, that's the thing..."

"What is the thing?"

"I, um, I've been saving up for school. Me and Mom both have." I took a breath, then rushed through the next part before I could change my mind. "But right now I don't have enough even for one year. It's close, but with the cost of rent and books and everything, I'm a little short. And I tried looking into student loans, but I can't get approved because of your, um, income. So I was wondering if you'd maybe help me with tuition. But I understand if that's too much, so I also checked into it and there's this statement you could fill out that says I'm not a dependent so I might qualify—"

"Absolutely not."

His words sliced through mine like a ribbon, so sudden and sharp and definitive that it took me a heartbeat before I processed them, despite my immediate silence.

"Oh," I said. "Okay. Well, thank you anyway. I'll figure something else out—"

"You will not be taking out *loans* for your education," he said, ignoring me. "And I most certainly will *not* be denying you as a dependent. I am shocked you would even think that I would consider saying you are not my daughter. What sort of person do you believe I am?"

My mouth was open, but the answer didn't come out. It didn't need to, though. My dad chuckled, though the sound was deliberate and sad.

"Of course." He sighed. "It is not your fault, *ma fille ange*. What your mother says is not up to you."

"She didn't say... I mean, I haven't told her about the... the option where you'd deny—"

"Nellie, keep your savings. You can use that for spending money. For fun things. Your tuition, your books, your—you said you need rent? Of course, since it is in Ottawa. All of that, you will not worry about. I will pay for it."

My voice shook and I tightened my blankets around me. "Even though I haven't been able to call or come to visit or...?"

It was a moment of careful consideration before he answered.

"You are an adult now," he said. "So I will not disrespect you and pretend it has not been very difficult not being able to see you or talk to you or spend time with you."

I swallowed hard. "That's fair."

"But you are still in high school. You are still living with your mother. You are still learning. So... perhaps if I cover these expenses, you can repay me."

"Like, instead of getting a loan?" I asked. "I'll pay you back once I, like, graduate?"

"No, no," he said. "I do not want money, *ma fille ange*. Never. All I would like is for you to spend some time here in Montreal. For you to visit. Perhaps for the summer and a few times throughout the school year, if that will work for you."

Oh my God.

Of course it worked.

I mean, it mostly did.

I'd have to figure out how to tell my mom.

She'd lose her mind if she found out about any of this. But a little white lie never hurt, right? So I could tell her I started looking at summer jobs in... well. Not in Ottawa and not in Montreal. But somewhere else. And I could tell her that if I worked the whole summer plus got a part time job while I was in school, it would cover the cost.

So maybe...

Maybe I just didn't tell her.

"*Ma fille ange*?" my dad said. "What do you think?"

"It's a deal, Dad."

Chapter Four
Good

"Ohmigod! *Chérie!*"

I winced at the high-pitched shriek, but Anne-Marie didn't notice. She was too busy nearly knocking me off the Marchands' front step and into the flower bed next to the door. Which would have been hilarious, seeing as it was the same flower bed I'd sunken into the very first day we'd met and declared ourselves best friends.

But it would have also sucked since I would've probably crushed Della Kinsley's geraniums with my ass instead of just leaving a butt-print in the wet dirt like I did when I was four.

So it was a good thing that Anne-Marie threw her long arms around me with reckless abandon, even if she was so excited that she didn't realize her height meant my face was stuffed against her boobs.

Which, like, no complaints. I was *pretty* sure I wasn't only into guys, but I wasn't ready to, like... explore that yet. Partly because I wasn't sure if I was thinking that because I was still mad about Adrian and didn't want to officially declare myself done with men. But mostly because I...

I don't know.

I just wasn't ready.

But either way, I wasn't offended that Anne-Marie shoved her boobs in my face, even if I wasn't into her like *that*. That wasn't to say she wasn't gorgeous. Gone was the gangly, freckled brunette she'd been as a child; the woman hugging me now was tall and slim and had cool-toned blonde hair that set off the warmth of her brown eyes and that no one who hadn't known her as a child would guess wasn't natural. Even though I had shown up on her doorstep unannounced, her makeup was flawless, foundation covering up any of the remaining freckles on her nose and contour applied so expertly that it was impossible to tell if the height of her cheekbones was an illusion.

It wasn't, for the record. She had the face and figure of a model. Fortunately or unfortunately, Anne-Marie was five-foot-seven-and-a-half, which made her too short for the modelling world.

So it wasn't that I didn't think she was attractive. I just had no romantic feelings for her whatsoever, even if she hadn't been dating her boyfriend, Remy, for nearly three years by that point.

"Hi, Anne-Marie," I choked after hugging her back and forcing my head back from her chest enough that I could speak.

"I didn't know you were coming! What are you doing here?"

"If you let go, I'll explain," I gasped.

She didn't let go right away, instead choosing to squeeze me one more time before untangling me from her arms. Even once she had, she kept a hand on me, as if I'd stop being real if she couldn't touch me.

"You had better start explaining, then," she demanded. "Because it has been *months*, Nellie."

"I know."

"Texting is not the same. Social media is not the same." She folded her arms across her chest. "Why did you not tell me you were coming?"

"Because I—" I stopped, frowning as I looked up at her and noticed her brown eyes were sparkling more than usual. "Wait, are you *crying*?"

She slapped my arm. "Months. I have not seen my best friend in, oh, what was it again? Oh yes. *Months*! Of course I am crying, dummy. When did you get here?"

"Barely half an hour ago," I said. "I wanted to surprise you. I literally pulled up, said hi to my dad and met his new girlfriend—"

"Ohmigod," Anne-Marie said immediately, lowering her voice. "What did you think of her?"

"She's..." I made a gesture with my hands that explained nothing and everything at the same time.

"Right?" Anne-Marie said. "Did you know, I heard she was trying to date men her own age but none of them want her because she is so impossible to deal with, so she began looking into older men. But when she was dating younger men, she tried to go out with Clinton Thibault."

I wrinkled my nose. "Ugh, don't tell me that. I don't want to feel bad for her. No one deserves a prick like him."

"Right, but Clinton is our age. She is twenty-five. And this was three years ago, so Clinton was fifteen at the time."

"Oh. Ew." I paused, then made a face. "How bad does someone have to be that I feel a little bad for Clinton Thibault?"

"Don't feel too bad for either of them. He turned her down."

I snorted. "I'm suddenly less annoyed that she already hates me."

Anne-Marie rolled her eyes. "She will not last long with your dad, I don't think."

I shrugged. "Anyway, after he introduced us, I brought a couple things to my room, then texted you. You're the first person other than them to know I'm in Montreal."

"As I should be," she said. "How long are you here until?" She gasped, her face brightening in realization. "You have not been here since you turned eighteen, *chérie*! If you are here until Friday, we can go to the bars together finally!"

"Well, actually—" I said, grimacing as if I had bad news.

Anne-Marie's face fell.

"—I'm here for the whole summer." I grinned. "We can go to the bars whenever we want."

She shrieked and from somewhere above us, I heard a muffled bang, but I was too busy being semi-suffocated by Anne-Marie again to pay much attention.

"The whole summer," she repeated, nearly bringing us to the ground as she shimmied in excitement. "This is just... it's so—"

She let go of me, but only because she fully started crying and had to wipe her eyes.

"Jeez, Anne-Marie," said a voice from the top of the stairs in front of us. "Are you being murdered or something? What is going on?"

She let out a dramatic sniffle, then rolled her eyes as she looked over her shoulder. "I am celebrating, Jean-Paul."

"Celebrating." Footsteps sounded on the stairs. "What the hell are you celebrating loud enough that I can hear you screaming from my room and—"

He stopped talking once he was in view of the front door, looked at me, then raised his eyebrows. "Nellie?"

And oh, *shit*.

Shit.

JP Marchand was obviously no longer a bossy nine-year-old boy with a missing tooth. That wasn't a surprise, of course; it wasn't like I hadn't seen him in the years since the Marchands moved in next door to my dad.

But I hadn't seen him for at least eight months, and now that I was thinking of it, I wasn't entirely sure I'd seen him the last time I'd been in Montreal, or even the time before that. I saw Anne-Marie almost every time I visited my dad, but it wasn't like I made a point to see JP. And my visits to my dad had been on long weekends whenever possible, which meant the last two times I'd seen him had been over Thanksgiving and Labour Day respectively.

And I'd been with Adrian, of course. So it wasn't like I was…
you know. *Looking* at him like… this. *And* JP was both Anne-Marie's
brother and a bossy wannabe lawyer who used to make fun of me and
Anne-Marie, so I wouldn't have ever—

I mean, I didn't have a crush on him.

Ever.

Obviously.

But I also wasn't blind.

So while I wasn't sure if I just hadn't looked at him like this because I'd
been with Adrian the last few times I'd visited Montreal or if something
had actually changed, JP seemed *completely* different.

The man standing on the stairs was both a walking stereotype and
disgustingly attractive. His face was all chiseled jaw and dazzling blue
eyes, his well-fitting jeans and polo shirt teasing a body that was all
angular muscles and tanned skin. To top it off, he had the kind of
highlighted blonde hair people would pay hundreds of dollars for in a
salon growing naturally from his big stupid head and a killer smile that
was showing off nice white teeth, though I was pleased to see that one of
them was a little crooked on the left side of his mouth.

But oddly enough, he was shooting that smile at me.

"See?" Anne-Marie said, wiping her eyes. "I have not seen Nellie since
last year. Of course I am excited."

"Of course," JP said. "Screaming bloody murder because your friend
is here is a sane and normal reaction." Anne-Marie stuck her tongue out
at him and he laughed. "How's it going, Nellie?"

Oh, God.

He was talking to me.

"Good," I said. "It's good. I'm good. Things are good."

"That's… good," he said.

"Yep. And you… Are you good?"

"Well, I haven't had any complaints," he said.

I blinked in confusion. "What?"

"Jean-Paul!" Anne-Marie said. "You pig!"

It took me a moment, but once he started laughing, I got it. My face turned red.

"I'm kidding," he said, shaking his head. "I'm doing good too, Nellie. Thanks for asking."

"Good." I winced as the word came out.

"Alright, well, I'm glad no one down here is getting murdered. I heard the door and thought maybe Anne-Marie was letting strangers in again." JP smiled and turned to go back upstairs. "Try to keep it down, would you?"

"We will not," Anne-Marie said. "Bye!"

He shook his head.

I think.

I mean, I saw movement in my peripheral that was probably him shaking his head or something, but those jeans of his were fitting really, uh...

You know.

Really good.

"So you still have a crush on my brother then?" Anne-Marie asked once the footsteps were no longer on the stairs.

"What?" I asked, my face flushing red. "Of course not. And what do you mean, *still*?!"

A puckish sort of smile flickered on her face before she giggled and looped her arm through mine to lead me to the living room so we could sit down. "Oh, no reason, of course. I assume all my friends have a crush on him."

"Ew. Why?"

The puckish smile turned into a patronizing look. "Nellie."

"What?" I wrinkled my nose. "Please don't tell me you think your brother is hot."

"Oh, good God," she said, sighing. "Of course not, *chérie*. This is not Alabama. I am just certain that at least three of my friends from school have been trying to sleep with him for the past few years. Though, I don't think he has done it with any of them. He may be a manwhore, but he is a manwhore who ensures his women are at least eighteen."

"Ah," I said, because what the fuck else was I supposed to say?

The bewilderment must have been clear on my face because Anne-Marie burst out laughing. "*Chérie*, Jean-Paul may be my brother, but I can understand that he is good-looking. I will question your sanity if you disagree."

"Well... yes," I admitted. "He is, like, objectively attractive. I guess."

"Oh, you *guess*," she repeated dismissively, holding in a laugh. "And he is also charming and well-off. The amount of women throwing themselves at him is concerning, if only for the fact that if his ego grows any larger, it may cause the second floor of the house to collapse. Since my bedroom is beside his, I am concerned I will be caught up in the disaster."

"I mean, you're also good-looking and charming and well-off," I said. "It's not like you're sleeping around with a bunch of his friends."

She laughed as we reached the couch and sat down. "Yes, but I could if I wanted to. Alas, I love my dear Remy. And"—she paused, leaning forward to make sure no one was in the nearby kitchen before continuing in a whisper—"he's made it known that there will be consequences if anyone tries to replace him."

The red flags started waving immediately. "Consequences?!"

She shook her head. "You are misunderstanding me, Nellie."

"Really? Because I'm hearing my friend tell me her boyfriend gives her consequences if someone tries to replace him and—"

She lifted a hand, trying to stop me. "It is not like that. It is all in fun. You have to remember, Remy and I have been dating for three years already. If we didn't, ah... play a little, I think things would get boring for us."

"Three years," I repeated, blinking at the realization. "And what do you mean, play? With who?"

"With each other's affections." She shrugged. "I do not want anyone else, but I do like knowing I'm desirable. And Remy, he likes feeling like he's earned me. It is nothing serious. I flirt a little and both of us know I would never actually do anything. He gets 'jealous' and both of us know he would not ever stop me from walking away if that was what I wanted. I trust him, you know? We have been together long enough that I *know* who he is. And he knows who I am."

A little stab of something regretful pricked in my chest at those words. Not because it was meant to be a dig. It wasn't. But it was a reminder that I didn't know Remy as well as I should.

That my best friend had been with her boyfriend for three *years* and almost everything I knew about him was through her because I'd only met him a handful of times. And of those times, only half were in situations where I could really get to know Remy, since the other half were the occasional galas or events my dad had me attend with him when I happened to be in town at the same time.

It was a reminder that my parents' divorce had uprooted everything for me. And worse, it was a reminder that after seven years, Anne-Marie was still my best friend.

Which sounded like a good thing. And it was. I was happy Anne-Marie was my best friend. But it was also a reminder that the girl who lived next door to my dad, a girl I hadn't seen in eight months and prior to that, had only seen a few times a year, was one of my *only* friends.

Especially after everything that happened with Adrian.

But it wasn't Anne-Marie's fault I was lonely. So while I wasn't entirely convinced that this was normal, since the idea of *playing* with someone's jealousy seemed outright insane, all I could do was trust that Anne-Marie knew what she was doing.

"If you say so," I said. "Just... be safe."

"I am, *chérie*." Her voice was gentle and appreciative. "I promise you, if either of us said we didn't want to do this anymore, we would stop, no problem. And if Remy ever so much as hinted that he might actually be angry or jealous, or if he started to show up when I've been serious about not wanting him to show up, we would be done. He knows that."

I couldn't stop myself from asking. "How?"

She thought for a moment, then shrugged. "It is something in how we talk about it, I think. Like, if I say no, and just *no*, that is no. And he knows that no is no."

I blinked at her, the words not quite hitting right. "O...kay."

"But if I say maybe something like 'I am going shopping with *mes chers* and don't you dare come find me when I am trying on lingerie at the shop you know I like on *rue Sherbrooke* and—"

"Okay," I said, far more quickly that time. "I get it."

She grinned. "And after we have our little play-arguments, the sex?" She pursed her lips, then pressed pinched fingers to her mouth and made a loud kissing sound. "*Magnifique*."

My cheeks went pink. "Oh. Good."

She made a sympathetic noise. "Still holding the v-card, *chérie*?"

"You know Adrian and I broke up," I said, not looking at her.

"Well, yes, but I find it very hard to believe you could not find someone else who would love to do the honours. You are one of the most beautiful girls I know."

The flattery made me turn fully red, though it was a happy kind of embarrassment. "Thanks, but also, no. I haven't been interested in dating anyone."

"Dating doesn't have to be a precursor," she said. "You don't even need to know the name of the person who pops it, *chérie*."

My jaw tightened and I stared hard at the other side of the room. After a moment of tense silence, Anne-Marie clapped her hand to her mouth and gasped in horror.

"Ohmigod. Nellie." She shook her head. "I am sorry. I wasn't thinking and—"

"It's fine," I said.

"*Chérie*, no, it is not. I am so, so sorry. The rumours—"

"—were rumours," I finished. "It's fine."

"It is not *fine*." She looked at me imploringly. "Even if the things he said were true, that is no reason for people to shame you the way they did. But it is also entirely understandable for it to be something that bothers you and—"

"I don't want to get into it," I said. "Like, I graduated. I don't have to see any of them ever again. I want to move on."

She nodded in understanding, then slipped her hand over mine. "You do not need to say a single word more. I will simply kill him if I ever meet him, *chérie*."

I laughed. "Thanks. You don't have to, though. I would hate for you to go to jail for me."

She waved her other hand nonchalantly. "My father is a lawyer. And Jean-Paul will be too, one day. And Remy, he thinks he wants to also go to law school. If between the three of them, they cannot prevent me from being imprisoned, then what even is the point of being related to lawyers?"

I frowned. "I didn't think your dad was a criminal lawyer."

"He's not. But it can't be all that difficult."

I had a feeling it was more difficult than she thought it was, but didn't say that. "Well, I appreciate the offer, but you don't need to kill Adrian on my behalf. I'm just... annoyed, I guess."

"About what?"

"That after all this, I'm still a virgin." I laughed, my face burning pink as I said the word out loud. "I was the one waiting for *him*. Like, just because we broke up doesn't mean that I don't want to... you know."

"So why not go out and find someone to do it with, then?" she asked.

I shrugged. "I guess after spending a semester with everyone calling me a slut and a whore and having school assemblies because of the shitstorm he caused, I don't want to just fuck any guy that walks across my path. I want to like the first guy I have sex with, you know?"

"You can like him. You don't have to love him."

"Yeah, but the first time should still be a little special."

"Nellie," she said with a laugh. "The first time is going to suck."

"It doesn't have to suck."

"But it will," she said. "My first time with Remy was terrible. Neither of us knew what we were doing, just that *this* part was supposed to go in *that* part and it should feel good. And I suppose it *was* wonderful... in its way. I am certain he enjoyed it, since he was inside for about six seconds before he pulled out and came all over my favourite Burberry skirt."

"You're selling it so well," I said.

"It got better, obviously. But if I could've gotten that first time over with some stranger so I didn't have to deal with Remy apologizing for the next hour while I tried to figure out how to clean cum off a wool skirt without my parents finding out, I probably would." She shrugged. "You also don't need to date someone for months and months before doing it. If you want to have sex, *chérie,* I can guarantee we will find you someone that you will both like and not have to bring home for Christmas."

"That's a pretty bold guarantee," I said, then twisted my mouth to the side as I considered it. "But... I mean, if you think we can make it happen..."

She gave me a look that was a mix of sass and playfulness, then propped her feet up on the coffee table. "If you want it to happen, then Eleanor Belanger, with God as my witness, we will make this the summer you lose your virginity."

Chapter Five
The Dude's Guide to Impressing Girls Online

HAD IT BEEN UP to Anne-Marie, I would've lost my virginity to one of the multiple eligible bachelors she said would be perfect for me.

"William is *gorgeous*," she said when we were sitting on her bed a few days later, showing me a picture of a guy who was, indeed, gorgeous. Unfortunately, William's dad was one of my dad's clients.

"I don't want it to be with someone where it'll get back to my dad," I said. "I mean, you know he's pretty Catholic."

"And the girlfriends he changes out every six months, they are all Catholic too, *chérie*?" she asked.

It was a good point, but pointing out that he was a hypocrite wouldn't help the situation. "Either way, I don't want to hook up with someone I might run into again at an event or a dinner party or something. My dad asked if I'd go to a couple of galas this summer, so chances are I'd have to see him again."

I think Anne-Marie thought I was being paranoid, but she gracefully agreed and swiped off William's social media profile.

"Gabriel, then," she said. "I am certain he does not know your father."

She twisted, reaching across the bed to show me her phone. I studied it for a moment, then frowned. "No way. That's Gabriel Marion."

"Huh?"

"I went to school with him. Like, before my mom and I moved."

"And that means he is not an option because…?"

"He smashed my *My Little Pony* lunch box in second grade and the lid broke off. I swore I'd never forgive him."

She gave me a *Look*. "Nellie."

I folded my arms. "I loved that lunch box."

She sighed, then swiped the screen and scrolled in silence for a few minutes.

"Antoine Chretien?" she suggested. I grimaced at the photo she showed me and she burst out laughing. "So he is not your type."

"I just can't with the fedora," I said.

"Reasonable." She held up her phone again. "Rene Masson is more your type, then?"

But he was also connected to my dad.

"It would have been nice to know that is an automatic veto," she grumbled.

"I'm not saying it's automatic," I said. "But I'd need him to be discreet about it. I don't know any of these guys well enough to trust them."

Anne-Marie made a soft huffing noise, a strand of blonde hair hanging over her face as she curled one leg beneath her, sitting on her foot and hanging her other leg off the edge of her bed. Her forehead was creased into a frown as she tapped her phone screen, determination setting her mouth into a flat line.

"You know you don't have to set me up, right?" I said. "I'm not looking for some long-term life partner here. Just something mostly casual with someone I won't regret hooking up with. I can download a dating app or—"

"*Ayoye!*" she gasped, clearly having not heard a word I said. "I have it, *chérie!*"

"Have what?"

"The perfect person for you to bequeath your v-card to." She shimmied in place as if she was too thrilled to stay still. "I know you will think he is attractive. And I can guarantee he does not want anything long-term, so you most certainly do not have to worry about him being clingy, even if you see him again. As for discretion? He will probably be ecstatic to have a clandestine hookup that you don't want anyone to know about, so long as it means he is getting laid."

I studied her suspiciously. "And who might that be?"

"Admit he sounds perfect," she said, clutching her phone to her chest.

Stubborn though I could be, I couldn't stand a mystery, which Anne-Marie knew well. "Fine. He sounds perfect."

The second the words were out of my mouth, she flipped her phone towards me, and the second I glanced at the screen, I knew who it was.

"God*damn*it, Anne-Marie!" I said.

"What?!" she asked, though she was giggling as she shoved the phone towards me as if seeing the photo more closely would change my mind. "He is the perfect option! And you will get to fulfill your lifelong dream—"

"I don't have a *lifelong dream* of hooking up with your *brother*," I hissed, snatching the phone away intending to turn the screen off.

But then I made the mistake of glancing down at it.

Even I had to admit it was a good photo of JP. He was wearing a greyish-blue suit, his blonde hair swept messily to one side and his tie loosened. There was a table of empty glasses in front of him and he was grinning, the crooked tooth on the side of his mouth peeking out. It had to be a trick of the camera, but I could've sworn there was a sparkle in his blue eyes, making it seem like he was staring straight through time and space so his gaze could meet mine.

"Are you certain, *chérie*?" Anne-Marie asked teasingly. "You are looking pretty hard at that photo, so—"

"I am not," I snapped, my face burning red. "I was looking at—"

JP's arm was slung around the person next to him, a man with black hair, dark reddish-brown skin and a semi-turned up nose who was also wearing a suit.

"—at his friend," I finished. "He's cute. Who's that?"

"His friend?" Anne-Marie reached out, taking the phone from me so she could see. "That's... *oh*." She grimaced, glancing up. "That's Samay. He went by Sam."

"Okay," I said. "And the problem is...?"

"*Went* by, Nellie," she repeated. "Before he, um, passed."

I blinked. "Oh. *Oh*."

She nodded, still cringing. "I just clicked on Jean-Paul's profile album and picked the nicest one, but he must have posted this, um..." She looked down at the phone and tapped the screen. "Two years ago, so yes. Around the time of the funeral. There was a bad car accident and he—well. He and JP went to college together. They were quite close."

I nodded along with her words, discomfort running through every inch of my body. "I didn't know."

"Of course not," she said. "I should have looked more closely at the photo I picked." There was another weird beat, then she smiled. "But what did you say before? About a dating app?"

We spent the next few hours filling out my profile and swiping through potential matches. Before long, I had an inbox full of messages, though most of them were just one or two words.

Or a picture the app said it was blurring for my own safety.

"This might have been a mistake," I said, my face turning red as I deleted another definitely-a-dick-pic. "This might've *definitely* been a mistake."

"It wasn't." She flopped forward, lying on her stomach as she took my phone from me. "You're just fresh meat on the app and all the desperate losers are shooting their shots. Once they're done, they'll make way for the better options. *Oh!*" She perked up gleefully. "Like this one!"

I peered over her shoulder to look at the screen.

> *I'm new at this, so bear with me, k?*

> *The Dude's Guide to Impressing Girls Online says to start with a unique but relatable question that shows off one of the perks of dating me and that you won't be able to resist answering.*

> *So: wanna steal my comfiest hoodie?*

And of course I responded.

> *Uh fuck yes I do*

> *Oh, shit! You replied! The Dude's Guide says this is good. Okay but there's a problem.*

> *Uh oh.*

> *Yeah. I have two really comfortable, fleecy, baggy hoodies. You want the navy blue one or the grey one?*

> *Grey, obviously. Everyone knows grey hoodies are the most comfortable.*

> *Got it ;) The Dude's Guide says I should be sure to wear that on our first date.*

Which, remind me again, is when?

Chapter Six
Kissing Cousins

"Would you look at you," Brayleigh said, a barely-veiled expression of contempt on her face as Anne-Marie and I came down the stairs the following Saturday.

I wish I could say it didn't surprise me, but it did. I looked at my dad to see if he'd noticed, but he was either ignorant or oblivious to Brayleigh's obvious judgement.

"She looks phenomenal, does she not?" Anne-Marie said, smiling prettily at Brayleigh in that "fuck you" kind of way she was so good at.

"That dress certainly... fits," Brayleigh said.

"You look nice, Nellie," my dad said diplomatically. "Where are you girls off to tonight?"

"Oh, I'm just going home," Anne-Marie said, wiping her hands on her jeans. "Nellie has a date."

And just like that, my dad's smile was gone and the warm cheerfulness of the foyer turned cold.

"A date?" he repeated, his voice stony. "I did not realize you were dating someone, Nellie."

"It's a first date," I said.

"A first date." He blinked, then an odd shiver of discomfort washed over me as he glanced down. "And you do not think you might give this young man the wrong idea, perhaps?"

I stared at him, stunned. "What?"

He raised his eyebrows. "Your... outfit."

Heat rushed up my face as I looked down at myself. I mean, I knew my dad was conservative, but I was wearing a *sundress*.

And yeah, it was Anne-Marie's sundress, which meant it was a little tight since she was tall and slim and I was shorter and curvier, but at most, it showed a bit more cleavage than I was used to. It wasn't like my boobs were hanging out.

Well, not *completely*.

"Is there a problem with her dress, Mr. Belanger?" Anne-Marie asked, her voice innocent. "She borrowed it from me. Since Nellie didn't really have anything similar to wear."

My dad glanced at her, his expression unchanged.

"That was very kind of you," Brayleigh said. "But perhaps Max is worried that the dress is a touch too revealing."

"Oh, not at all!" Anne-Marie said, her voice bright. "I have worn this dress to church before. But thank you for the concern! It is nice that you care for Nellie so much, Brayleigh."

My dad's jaw twitched almost imperceptibly. "And who is this date with? Is it anyone I know?"

"Uh, his name is Tyson," I said uncertainly. "We're just getting to know each other."

"*Just* getting to know each other?" He raised his eyebrows. "How did you meet him, then?"

"Online," I said.

"Online." The word came out flat and unimpressed. "Hmph. And what does he do for work?"

"He's a student."

"What do his parents do for work?"

"I don't know." I frowned. "It's a first date, Dad. I don't know if I'll even want to go out with him again."

He nodded briskly, once, his mouth tightening. "And when will you be home?"

"Uh…" I glanced at Anne-Marie. "I mean, we're just going for a few drinks and—"

"I expect that you will return home tonight," he said in a clipped voice. "Do you understand, Eleanor?"

I did. Very well. And I very confidently told him that I *would* be returning home that night.

Because even though I'd been enjoying talking with Tyson and getting to know him, I'd already decided I wasn't going to hook up with him right away. Not wanting a serious relationship didn't mean I wanted to jump into bed with him immediately; I still wanted my little bit of special, however that happened to be.

I'd worried that might be hard to find. That finding someone who didn't want something serious, was willing to wait at least a date or two to hook up, and was also willing to make things special wouldn't exist, despite Anne-Marie's insistence that he would.

But after I walked into the bar to find Tyson sitting there in a grey zip-up hoodie, I thought maybe I'd worried for nothing.

"Tyson?" I asked as I approached the table.

He looked up from his phone, a half-smile on his face, then blinked in surprise as he stared at me.

"Holy—wow." He shook his head slowly. "The Dude's Guide did *not* have advice for what to do when your date walks in looking like a freaking *goddess*."

I burst out laughing. "Did The Dude's Guide tell you to say that even if she showed up wearing a paper bag?"

His mouth curled into a smile. "Well, it *did* suggest complimenting her outfit no matter what, but this is just... damn." He looked down at his hoodie. "I feel underdressed compared to you."

"Well, there's an easy way to fix that," I said.

His eyebrow twitched up. "Is there?"

"Yeah. I'm stealing your hoodie so I can dress this down a bit."

He stood up instantly, unzipped the hoodie, and shrugged it off to reveal a black t-shirt before holding it out to me.

Which was a mistake on his part.

Not because I was going to steal his hoodie. I wasn't actually planning on taking it home with me.

And not because putting his hoodie on covered up the exquisite view he had of my cleavage. I left the zipper undone because Tyson hadn't requested I keep it down so he could stare at my boobs, and I figured that deserved the reward of being able to stare at my boobs.

No, it was a mistake because Tyson sealed his fate by letting me wear it.

"—so then we drove down to Ottawa," Tyson was saying. I was two margaritas in with a laugh on my lips and butterflies in my stomach, secretly wondering how I was going to keep myself from actually going home with him that night because we were hitting it off so well. "And after we got there, my buddy goes—"

"*Salopard*!" someone screeched from behind me.

Tyson stopped talking, his face going white as he looked past me.

"Wait," he said. "Wait, I—"

"Tyson Roy, *tas de merde*, how fucking *dare* you?!"

The bar nearly went silent and my mouth dropped open as a chubby woman with curly brown hair and olive-toned skin stormed up to our table.

It wasn't like I didn't figure out what was going on immediately. I knew. Fucking everyone knew. But I still looked from him to the woman, the dread in my stomach begging for another explanation.

"Who are you?" I asked.

"Who am I?" she shouted, patches of red appearing on her cheeks. "I am Celine. Who are *you*?!"

"I'm—"

"My cousin," Tyson said quickly.

"Your cousin?" Celine repeated as I snapped my head towards him, outraged. "And she's sitting there in your favourite hoodie because...?"

"It's not what it looks like." Tyson shot me a pleading look. "She was cold. Right, cuz?"

"I'm not your *cousin*!" I spat.

He looked up at the ceiling. "Godda—"

"Good," Celine spat. "I am ashamed to be your girlfriend in the first place, but this would be far worse if she was your cousin, you inbreeding *freak*."

"Will you let me explain?" he said.

"Explain *what*?" Celine and I asked at the same time.

"Exactly," Celine said. "Unless you are going to explain how one can be so stupid, I don't think there is much that I cannot figure out myself."

"Or you could also explain why you're online dating when you have a girlfriend," I said.

"He does not have one anymore," Celine said.

I shoved my chair back from the table. It hit the floor with a bang. "I can't believe you did this. Especially to *her*."

"I didn't do anything!" he said defensively. "You and I, we never did anything—"

"We were gonna," I said, folding my arms and glaring at him.

"I knew it." Celine's voice cracked. "I *knew* you were going to do something like this. Everyone warned me but I was so sure they were wrong. I'm so stupid."

"You are *not* stupid," I said to her. "He's stupid. He had a girlfriend as hot as you and he's going around cheating on her? There are slugs with higher IQs than him."

"I never cheated!" Tyson insisted. "She's lying, Celine! She's my cousin but she hates me so—"

I picked up my half-finished margarita and jerked the glass forward. The frozen slush splashed out, hitting Tyson directly in the face.

"Mother*fuc*—"

"*Tabarnak*," Celine said. "I wanted to do that."

"You still can," I said, then leaned over and reached across the table to grab Tyson's beer. "Here."

He'd just finished brushing lime slush out of his eyes when a wave of IPA drenched his face and t-shirt. Celine set the glass down on the table loudly.

"Thank you," she said.

"No problem. I'm sorry you had to find out he's a cheating bastard." I glared at Tyson, who was sputtering.

"Don't be. I am sorry I ruined your date." She sighed. "And you are dressed up so cute, too."

"I mean, I don't think you need to apologize for saving me from this rat." I folded my arms. "But also, I'm all dressed up and you probably need a drink. Wanna go get one together?"

"Yes," she said. "Let's go. He can get the bill."

"Can I at least get my hoodie back?" Tyson called as Celine and I turned to leave.

In unison and without looking back, the two of us lifted our middle fingers, then looped our arms together and walked out.

Chapter Seven
Giving Up

"I give up," I said a few weeks later.

Anne-Marie and Celine looked up from the lattes sitting in front of them.

"You are here early," Celine said, frowning. "Why are you giving up?"

"And... *chérie*, what happened to my dress?" Anne-Marie added, her brow furrowing as I pulled a chair over from an empty table nearby.

"It's covered in melted cheese grease."

She exchanged looks with Celine. "I thought you were going for a walk at the Old Port."

"I was. And apparently, Patrick thought he might get hungry, so he packed himself a snack. But where you or I may grab a protein bar or an apple or something, he decided the best snack to bring was a thermos of melted cheese."

"A *thermos* of melted cheese?" Celine repeated. "A *thermos*?!"

"Mm-hmm. And some bread. I think maybe he was trying to do a fondue-on-the-go type of thing. But when he opened it, a bunch of grease spilled out and he lost his grip on the container, so he managed to spill the entire thing down the front of my dress."

"You mean my dress," Anne-Marie said, though she was laughing. "Oh, *chérie*. How does this keep happening to you?"

Technically, it was the first time this particular thing had happened to me, but I knew what she meant.

The past month had been an absolute disaster. First, there was the whole Tyson thing. Though, that ended up working out since Celine and I ended up hitting it off. After spending the night rage-drinking in a bar a few blocks away from where I'd met up with Tyson, I apparently invited her to brunch with Anne-Marie the next day.

I didn't fully *remember* inviting her, but that was fine. She and Anne-Marie hit it off immediately and when I woke up after stumbling home to sleep off far too many mimosas for someone as hungover as I was, the three of us had a group chat dedicated to the mission of finding me someone to hook up with. And somehow, my experience with Tyson hadn't completely turned me off the world of online dating, so the following week, I went out for drinks with a guy named Nolan.

Well, I say drinks. I had one drink, then said I had a stomachache. Which was true because I was already sick of hearing about the ex-girlfriend he was clearly still hung up on.

After Nolan was Philippe, who scoffed and rolled his eyes when I told him my French was a bit rusty because even though I'd grown up in Montreal, my first language was English since my mom hadn't spoken French, and then I'd spent the last seven years in Toronto. Unfortunately for him, I understood French better than I spoke it, so when he took a call in the middle of our date and started calling me *"une pute anglophone,"* I got up and left.

After Philippe came Simon, who was *very* into cryptocurrency. And then there was Isaac—or, rather, there *wasn't* Isaac, who messaged me to say he was walking into the bar, but when I looked up so he could see where I was sitting, he had already disappeared.

And now Patrick, who ruined my borrowed sundress with a bunch of melted cheese, then refused to apologize because he thought the cheese smelled better than my perfume.

"He did *not*," Anne-Marie said, cackling.

"I'm not even wearing perfume," I muttered.

Celine sipped her coffee. "You will not find someone online that fits what you're looking for, Nellie."

"I'm realizing that."

"We could try going out to the clubs again," Anne-Marie said.

"That's had an even worse track record," I said.

"That is because you are going to the wrong clubs," Celine said in a sing-song voice.

"We are going to perfectly good clubs," Anne-Marie said. "Just because you think dive bars are good hunting grounds for men of quality—"

"Les Bleus is not a dive bar," Celine said. "But you keep going to these high-end nightclubs that only fuckboys who think they are God's gift to women go to and then are surprised when the men are all fuckboys."

"They are not *all* fuckboys."

"Certainly, but considering the rest are the fuckiest of boys, it averages out to an entire club of fuckboys."

"And I am sure Les Bleus is not completely full of slimy garbage, but since the majority are the *slimiest* of garbage—"

It was one of the few things Anne-Marie and Celine didn't agree on. Anne-Marie took it as a personal insult that Celine didn't like the nightclubs she liked. But Celine had a point; Anne-Marie kept taking us to the kinds of clubs frequented by the children of parents with too much money, taking shot after shot of Patron and slugging Dom Perignon straight from the bottle in an attempt to feel something for once.

Not that I didn't understand why Anne-Marie was insulted. The people at those clubs were *her* people. Every time we went out, we would run into someone she knew from one social club or another, or who she went to college with, or who frequented the same charitable events Anne-Marie attended. And Celine didn't exactly hold back her opinions about the "*fuckboys et pouffiasses*" that made up those groups of people.

So it made sense that Anne-Marie was offended, even though she wasn't like all those *fuckboys et pouffiasses*. She could be out-of-touch and almost silly at times, but beneath it all, she was a good person.

But it didn't change that the clubs Anne-Marie liked were full of guys wearing too much cologne beneath a tacky designer shirt, asking every girl they met for nudes before buying them a drink, and performing a complex mating dance that included rubbing their dick on the asses of every girl in the club unfortunate enough to be looking the other direction.

And yet, I'd still given my phone number to a couple of the least-offensive-seeming guys in the hopes that we could meet up some other time. But aside from one who texted me at three a.m. on a Tuesday a week and a half later asking if I was up and wanted to Netflix and chill, I hadn't heard from any of them.

"Because fuckboys are looking for someone to fuck right then, right there, with no strings attached," Celine said, breaking me out of my thoughts in the weirdest, most relevant way. "And that is not what Nellie is looking for."

Anne-Marie sighed. "This would be so much easier if it was, though."

"My apologies for making your life difficult," I said dryly.

She gave me an unimpressed look. "*Chérie*, you are overcomplicating this. You want sex, have sex. You're putting unnecessary pressure on yourself to have it be someone who fits all these standards."

"So I shouldn't have standards," I said.

She rolled her eyes. "That is not what I said. But it is like you have a goal and are fighting yourself on it for no good reason."

"That is not fair," Celine said. "Nellie has every right to pick the exact right person to do this with. But while she *is* too hot for her own good, even she won't be able to find the kind of person she's looking for at a place like Club Lumina."

"I'm starting to think it's because the person I'm looking for doesn't exist," I said.

"Well, that is possible, too," Celine said.

"He most certainly does exist," Anne-Marie said. "You're just being stubborn about it."

"Being stubborn about what?" I asked, frowning.

"Jean-Paul."

I made an aggravated noise. "JP is not an option, Anne-Marie."

"Who is JP?" Celine asked.

"Her brother," I said.

"Her childhood crush," Anne-Marie said at the same time.

I rolled my eyes. "I don't have a crush on him."

"Mmm. And I don't smell the sharp scent of melted cheddar all over you."

"Is he hot?" Celine asked.

"No," I said, then turned to Anne-Marie. "Why are you so obsessed with me hooking up with your brother?"

"Because it would be cute," she said. "And I've always wanted a sister. When I discovered Marc-Andre had a penis, I yelled at my mother for letting him come out too early because I thought if he was in her belly longer, it would fall off and he would turn into a girl."

It was a hot minute before Celine and I stopped laughing long enough that I could keep talking.

"Okay, but even if I did hook up with JP, I wouldn't be your sister," I said. "The whole point of this is that I don't want to get into a relationship with someone."

"Yes, but who's to say what happens after you fuck? Maybe you end up liking each other," Celine said. "I bet you that's what Anne-Marie is hoping for."

Anne-Marie shushed her. "Don't *tell* her that! Now she will never have sex with my brother."

I shuddered. "You talk about this way too casually for someone you are biologically related to."

"It is a little weird," Celine said. "But it also proves a point."

"What point?" I asked.

"Well, it stands to reason that if JP exists, then so does an actual perfect candidate who isn't your friend's brother," she said. "I mean, I'm sure he's nice and all, but he can't possibly be one in a million."

"He thinks he is," Anne-Marie said. "But so do the, what is it, seven or eight thousand others in the world who also think they're one in a million?"

"Which means there are probably four or five of him in Montreal alone," Celine continued. "So you don't have to give up, like you said when you walked in. You can keep trying. And *maybe* if you consider trying somewhere that doesn't have valet parking full of Lamborghinis and McLarens, you will find him."

"Yes, instead of valet parking, Les Bleus has complimentary syringes and crack spoons," Anne-Marie said. "And if the paramedics that show up after someone ODs manage to bring them back to life, they owe the entire bar a round."

Celine rolled her eyes. "Just because the people at Les Bleus don't have wine cellars full of aged Grey Poupon or whatever it is you rich people waste your money on doesn't mean it's a crack den, Anne-Marie."

"I think it would be called a mustard cellar in that case, not a wine cellar," I said.

"I just do not see how you expect Nellie to find a decent, respectful man to pop her cherry with at a place that someone has almost certainly been stabbed at," Anne-Marie said.

"Because searching for a lover amongst the fuckboys has been so very fruitful," Celine said. "And no one has been *stabbed* at Les Bleus, at least not recently. And you know what, even if that happened, maybe Nellie is destined to have sex with the cute paramedic who shows up to help them."

"She's got a point," I said.

"I know I do," Anne-Marie said.

"Not you." I gestured at Celine. "*She* has a point."

Anne-Marie looked at me, horrified. "You want to go to Les Bleus?"

"What's the worst that can happen?" I said.

"We get stabbed," Anne-Marie said, her voice pitching up.

"Well, in a way, that's kind of what Nellie is hoping for, isn't it?" Celine said.

I snorted so loudly that at least three people at other tables shot dirty looks our direction. Anne-Marie sighed heavily, then shook her head in defeat.

"Fine," Anne-Marie said. "We can go tonight. But if one single person offers me heroin, we are leaving."

"No one's going to offer you heroin," Celine said. "Maybe cocaine, but the only difference between that and Club Lumina is that at Les Bleus, they'd ask you to pay for your share and snort it off the toilets instead of the bar top while the bartender looks the other way."

We finished our coffees and agreed to meet Celine at Les Bleus that night, then Anne-Marie and I headed back home. After having dinner with my dad and Brayleigh, I grabbed my makeup and walked over to the Marchands'. Anne-Marie and I had gotten into the habit of getting ready to go out at her place, since if my dad had reacted the way he did to the slightly-low-cut-but-overall-relatively-modest sundress I'd been wearing out for dates, he would lose his mind at the sight of what I was wearing to the bars.

Most of the time, I borrowed something from Anne-Marie. Between regularly attending galas and luncheons and other high society type events, having two parents who were decidedly more liberal when it came to fashion, and the fact that the drinking age in Quebec was lower than it was in Ontario, she had a much larger collection of dresses and skirts and low-cut tops than I did. That night, she lent me a glittery mesh charcoal grey number that already clung to my curves before emphasizing them with ruching that went up the sides. I let her curl my hair, then did my makeup while waiting for her to finish curling her hair so I could do her makeup, too.

"Oh, one thing before we leave, *chérie*," Anne-Marie said once we were ready, stopping me as we stepped out of her bedroom to go downstairs.

"What?" I asked distractedly, tugging the skirt of the dress down since it was already starting to ride up my thighs. "Also, I dunno if this is gonna work. I might need to change—"

"I know you and Celine think I am being crazy, but regardless, I have asked someone to accompany us to and from the bar," she said, ignoring me. "You know. For safety."

I stopped tugging on my skirt, then took a tentative couple of steps to see if it would stay in place. "I told you Remy can come out with us whenever he wants as long as it's clear he's with *you* so I can keep trying to meet someone. Are we Ubering with him or is he meeting us there?"

"Mmm, no," she said. "Not Remy. He is out of town this weekend. And we're not Ubering tonight."

I frowned, looking up at her. "What? Are you not drinking tonight?"

"No, I am."

"Well, *I'm* not driving."

She laughed. "I know. I got us a designated driver so we will not have to wait for a ride there or risk being stabbed while waiting for a ride back."

"What? Who?"

Anne-Marie just smiled. Then, with her eyes still on me, she knocked on the closed door next to her bedroom. I stared at it, then looked back at her as betrayal rushed through every inch of my body.

"You have got to be kidding—"

The door opened and JP walked out looking effortlessly gorgeous in a red McGill hoodie and those fucking jeans that fit him so goddamn good.

"Is this my sign that you two are finally ready to go?" JP asked.

Chapter Eight
Reds and Bleus

I KNEW I'D MADE a mistake when we walked into Les Bleus and the first thing I saw was a shot glass sticking out of a man's ass.

He was face down on top of the bar, navy blue sweatpants pulled down to his knees and his feet in the air, kicking lazily back and forth like a teenage girl daydreaming about her crush. Tucked into his ass crack was a shot glass full of bright blue liquid. Behind the bar, a bored-looking bartender had his arms folded across his chest as another bartender held up her phone.

"Okay!" she shouted, her voice loud enough that I could hear it over the pounding music. "Legs down, *monsieur*!"

The man stopped kicking his feet and put his legs flat on the bar.

"Excellent." The bartender lifted an arm in the air and held up three fingers. "Three! Two! One! *Go!*"

"What is going o—*OHMIGOD!*" Anne-Marie nearly slapped herself in the face as she clapped a hand to her mouth. On the other side of me, Celine dissolved into laughter, and I stared with wide eyes as a petite woman hopped onto the bar, straddled the back of the man's thighs, and shoved her face against his ass. She shook her head to the left and then the right and a moment later, sat back on her knees with her head tilted all the way back. A trail of blue liquid dripped down her chin as she lifted her hand to pull the now-empty shot glass out of her mouth.

"Time!" the bartender holding the phone said. "You have tonight's new record!"

"And that's how you do it, Edouard!" the woman on the bar screamed, pointing at someone nearby before throwing the shot glass on the ground. It shattered and the bored-looking bartender sighed, shaking his head before turning around and grabbing a broom and dustpan.

"That should not count. He is *way* less hairy than Joel!" said the man, who was apparently Edouard. "I am going to be picking ass hair from my teeth for a month!"

"Welcome to Les Bleus!" Celine said cheerfully.

"You know, I bet Jean-Paul hasn't even left the parking lot yet," Anne-Marie said, leaning towards me. "If we leave now, I bet we could still get into Vivre without even having to wait..."

But there was no chance in hell of that happening.

Especially when I knew JP was for *sure* still in the parking lot.

"Would you like to repeat that?" JP had said when Anne-Marie told him where he was taking us. He gave her an incredulous look through the rear-view mirror since she had oh-so-kindly *insisted* I sit in the front seat of JP's black BMW.

"Les Bleus," Anne-Marie repeated, buckling her seatbelt. "Nellie can get the directions, if you like, since it was her idea."

"You're getting me to drop you off at Les Bleus," he said. "In a BMW." Then glanced at me. "Dressed like that?"

I glared at him, offended. "What's wrong with how I'm dressed?"

He smirked. "Look, if you're going to Les Bleus to pick up someone, I'm pretty much legally obligated to tell you that's a bad idea. Especially dressed like you're going to a place with bottle service and a twenty-five-dollar cover."

Anne-Marie rolled her eyes. Or at least, I think she did. Her tone of voice sounded like it accompanied an eyeroll. "You do not know what you're talking about, Jean-Paul. If we look hot, it does not matter if we're overdressed."

"You don't think so?" he asked.

"How would you even know?"

"You don't think I've been to Les Bleus?"

"I don't think you know what it's like to pick up guys at bars."

"Oh, and you're the expert?"

"It's fine," I said, interrupting both of them. "We're not going to pick anyone up. Anne-Marie is with Remy and I'm not going home with someone tonight."

JP made a knowing noise. "So you're being a tease."

I made an offended noise. "How am I a tease?!"

He flicked his eyes down, then raised one eyebrow. "Come on, Nellie. You're not that naïve."

My face *burned*. "If you think my clothes are an invitation, you're a bastard."

Infuriatingly, he laughed. "I'm not saying they are. I *am* saying that if you don't want to run into people who do think that, maybe you should consider somewhere else. What about Vivre? It's pretty fun."

"We're meeting our friend," I said.

He shrugged. "Have it your way. To Les Bleus it is."

"What, you don't think we can handle ourselves?"

JP looked at me from the corner of his eye, a smirk on his lips. "I may just go get myself an Iced Capp instead of heading home, since I'm giving it twenty minutes before you call begging me to pick you up."

I folded my arms across my chest and looked stubbornly out the window. "I'd never beg you for anything."

"We'll see about that," he murmured.

"*Waouh*, you two," Anne-Marie said from the back seat. "Get a room."

My face went bright red, JP burst out laughing, and I spent the rest of the drive to Les Bleus with my jaw clenched and arms folded, one leg crossed over the other as I stared out the window like the road would disappear if I wasn't watching it.

So we weren't leaving. No matter how much JP didn't think I could handle myself at a place like this. Or how obvious it was that Anne-Marie wanted to leave not only because she didn't want to be here but because it would give her even more of a chance to push me and JP together like we were two Barbie dolls she was trying to make kiss.

"We're not going to Vivre," I said to Anne-Marie as the man lying on the bar struggled to get to his knees without exposing his dick to everyone in the bar. "Why would you want to? All the life is happening in this place."

"That's the spirit!" Celine hooked her arm through mine. "Let's go get a drink. Don't worry, they do not serve them all out of men's ass cracks. Although, you *do* get a hundred dollars if you are the fastest of the night to jump on the bar and finish your shot."

"Do they just give you some random guy or do you get to pick who you do the shot off of?" I asked as we reached the bar.

"Either," she replied.

I hummed thoughtfully, tilting my head to the side. "Well then, maybe."

"You cannot be serious, *chérie*!" Anne-Marie said, her eyes going wide with disgust. "Why would you want your face that close to anyone's ass? And you don't even know when the last time they showered was!"

"It would be one hell of a story about her first time," Celine said with a giggle.

"There is such a thing as too much of a story, you know," Anne-Marie said.

And unfortunately, she may have been more right about that than I'd like to admit.

We started by ordering a couple of drinks each and wandering around Les Bleus, getting a feel for the layout and the people there.

And those people were… well.

"See anyone you might be interested in?" Anne-Marie asked after I watched a guy reach into the waistband of his sweats—since the guy on the bar was not the only person who showed up to the bar in sweatpants—and scratch himself, then pull his hand out and sniff his fingers.

"A few options," I said, trying to sound as positive and assured as I could. "But anyone wearing sweatpants is off the table."

"Well, that will take doing a butt shot off the table, too," Celine said. "The ones in sweatpants are most likely to do one since it is easier to… you know." She mimed pulling her pants down. "At least one of them will probably ask if you want to fuck in the bathroom for the same reason."

I tried to laugh. Anne-Marie looked at me, amused.

"Vivre?" she said.

I scoffed. "No way. Let's get another drink and go dance."

And that had seemed promising. It really had. A song or two after we got on the dance floor, a normal looking guy wearing jeans and an unstained t-shirt made eye contact with me. I raised my eyebrows at him and he flicked his eyes up and down my body, then smiled and started to work his way through the crowd of people towards me.

"Oh my God," I said, trying not to move my lips because he was still looking at me. "Guys. Guys! I think I found a normal person."

"Where?" Anne-Marie whirled around.

"Him?" Celine asked, still moving her body in time to the beat as she leaned in so I could hear her.

"Uh-huh."

"He's cute," she said.

"Very," Anne-Marie said almost begrudgingly.

I took a sip of my drink as I watched him, my heart pounding in time to the thundering bass of the music. He slipped between two groups of people, then looked away from me for a moment to apologize to someone he'd run into.

A moment later, he was in front of me, a smile on his lips as he opened his mouth.

"Hey," I said over the music. "I'm—"

And then it was like a truck hit me.

"*Putain de merde!*" Anne-Marie cursed, grabbing me before I fell to the floor but not before I doused both her and myself with the half-empty vodka cranberry in my hand.

"Hey!" Celine shouted. "*C'est quoi ça, tabarnak!*"

The girl who had bodychecked me out of the way shot her a dirty look, then shouted something in French so rapid and so slurred that I couldn't tell what she said. Celine's face went red and she started shouting back, but Anne-Marie grabbed her arm.

"Not worth it!" she said. "Come on, before the stain sets and Nellie ruins three of my dresses today."

"It's not my fault," I said as she pulled me towards the edge of the dance floor, icy cranberry juice dripping down my legs.

"I know it is not, *chérie*." She was trying not to laugh, even as Celine fumed beside her, a river of mumbled curses still running from her mouth. "But trust me, that man was not good-looking enough for you to get into a physical fight with some crazy bar star."

"What was her problem?" I asked, but a quick glance behind me answered before Anne-Marie did. The guy who had approached me was looking at the girl with raised eyebrows, then shrugged and put his hands on her hips. She pressed her body against his and tilted her head so she could find out what the back of his throat tasted like.

"She was interested in the same man you were," Celine said as we reached the bar.

"I didn't even do anything," I said. "I didn't even *talk* to him."

Anne-Marie was still laughing as she reached over the bar and helped herself to a stack of napkins, then held half of them out to me. "Time for us to go to Vivre, then?"

I rolled my eyes and snatched the napkins from her. "Why would we go to Vivre? This is fine. We're having fun."

"Are we?" she asked.

I dabbed at my dress. "It's a minor inconvenience at best. And we'll have some great stories to tell about tonight."

"I thought we were here to find someone for you to fuck, not collect great stories," Anne-Marie said.

"Yeah, but—"

"Well, if *that's* the case"—I stumbled forward as a heavy arm flumped across my shoulders, a garbled man's voice interrupting me unexpectedly —"may I offer my services, sweetheart?"

I didn't even need to look at the man to know I wasn't interested. I mean, I did, but Celine's expression was written in whatever the facial equivalent of capital letters is. He was about my age and seemed to be an average weight, though he was quite a bit taller than me. He was wearing sweatpants, because of course he was, and had a lewd grin on his face showing off a bad set of veneers. His breath reeked of beer and I had to wonder if that was all he'd been drinking because it seemed too damn early in the night for him to be *that* drunk.

"That's gonna be a pass from me," I said.

The man laughed. "Aw, come on, baby. You're not even gonna give me a chance?"

"You're not my type," I said.

He scoffed. "How am I not your type?"

"I have a no-sweatpants rule."

He laughed loudly, pulling me against his body. "Don't worry. I'll take 'em off first."

I grimaced. "It's still a no. Let go of me, please."

"One kiss," he said. "Give me a kiss and I bet you change your mind."

"I can't," I said. "I'm, uh... I'm gluten intolerant and I can tell you've been drinking beer."

He tilted his head thoughtfully. "That's fair. What if I brush my teeth?"

"Dental hygiene is always a good idea," Anne-Marie said. "You should go do that."

Surprisingly enough, he let go of me. "I'll come back for you, sweetheart."

He walked away—well, it was more of a lurch away, I guess—and I exchanged looks with Celine.

"I can't believe that worked," I said.

"Perhaps it is time for us to call Jean-Paul, *chérie*," Anne-Marie said.

I made an aggravated noise. "We're not letting one creepy guy ruin the night. Let's get another drink and go to the other side of the bar to avoid him."

"But—" she started.

"He will not even remember talking to us," Celine said to Anne-Marie. "It is fine. I will watch out for her."

But neither of those things were true.

It wasn't Celine's fault. We'd found an out-of-the-way corner of the bar to set up in so we could keep an eye out for the creepy guy. Anne-Marie was the one who decided she had to go to the bathroom and insisted she would go by herself, even though girl code was clear about going to the bathroom in groups.

"We do not want to lose this spot," she shouted over the music. "And I need someone to watch my drink. I will be fine, *chérie*."

She'd only been gone for a couple of minutes when someone shouted and came out of nowhere to throw their arms around Celine, who screeched and hugged her back.

"Juliette!" she shouted. "*Mon dieu*! It has been so long!"

I sipped my drink, scanning the bar as Celine caught up with her friend, who was apparently someone she'd gone to college with. So I didn't notice when Celine wandered away to say hello to the other friends who were at the bar. And it wasn't like she went *far*, but it was far enough that she didn't notice when the creepy sweatpants guy tracked me down.

"There you are, sweetheart," he said, suddenly appearing in my line of sight.

I startled, nearly spilling my drink on myself again. "Oh. Uh... hi."

He flashed that creepy grin, the whiteness of his veneers unnatural in the dim corner of the bar. "They had mouthwash n' everything in the bathroom. So I'm minty clean, baby. Wanna get out of here?"

"No," I said.

He just grinned even wider, taking a step forward. "I get it. A little rendezvous in the bathroom is more your speed?"

"Definitely not," I said. "I'm not interested."

That didn't deter him. "It's okay to be nervous, sweetheart. But I promise I'll make it good for you. We'll have a good time together, yeah?"

"No," I said yet again, but he took another step towards me. Which was...

I mean, I was annoyed more than anything. Until I glanced around looking for someone who could help me and realized that whole thing where I was in an out-of-the-way corner of the bar was no longer a *good* thing. I wasn't quite trapped, but I also wasn't going to be able to get past him without being close enough that he could grab me or something. And no one was paying enough attention to that little corner that I could flag them down without him realizing what I was doing.

"Playing hard to get?" the man said.

"I... no," I said, my heart racing. "I'm just... I can't."

"I think you can," he said.

"Nope. I'm... on my period."

He gestured dismissively. "I'm washable."

"Yeah, well"—I glanced in the general direction I'd last seen Celine, then around for *anyone* that might be watching—"I also have a boyfriend."

He took another step towards me. "You don't."

"What?" I said. "Yes, I do."

He laughed. "You would've said that first if you did."

"Well, maybe I didn't think you were the kind of asshole who only respected what women said if another guy had already claimed them."

"Sweetheart, there's no way you have a boyfriend," he said. "And if you did, he would be doing a shit job of it, letting you be out at the bar dressed like this all by yourself."

I saw red.

Not because I was mad. I mean, I was absolutely furious, enough that I forgot I was trying to be careful because upsetting a persistent guy in the corner of a bar might make things worse and opened my mouth to snap back that no man *let* me do anything.

But I *literally* saw a familiar shade of red fabric in my peripheral vision as a tall frame moved beside me, a casual but comforting hand resting on the middle of my back.

"Trust me, man," JP said, his amusement clear even over the pounding music. "I don't *let* her do anything. She can do whatever she wants."

Oh God.

Oh my *God*.

The other man stared at JP, the grin sliding off his face until all that remained was a cold, annoyed expression. "Bullshit."

"Excuse me?" JP said.

"If you're her boyfriend, why's she running around trying to find other guys to hook up with?" he said.

"Mmm, I dunno about that," JP said, his voice light. "It sounded like she wasn't interested and you weren't taking the hint."

The man scoffed. "Trust me, if she wasn't gluten intolerant, I'd already have fucked your girl."

JP reacted like that made total sense. "Well, I guess you missed out then."

The other man rolled his eyes before looking at me. "Seriously? You're gonna go home with a fucking pretty boy like him? I bet he won't even get with you during shark week."

I wasn't sure if JP thought the guy was really passionate about the Discovery Channel or if he figured out I'd tried to claim I was on my period so the guy would leave me alone, but either way, he didn't address it. "C'mon, babe. Let's go."

"She's coming with me," the man said, reaching for me. "I'll even go down on you, sweetheart."

I saw red again. Mainly because JP put his arm between me and the man, followed by the rest of his body, so all I could see was the back of his hoodie.

"The fuck, man?" I heard the other man say. "Get out of my fucking—"

From somewhere on my left, there was a loud shout that cut the man off, and it seemed like half the bar turned to look at the source.

"—say dat about my mudder, ya piece of shit!" someone was screaming in a loud Newfoundland accent. JP moved just in time for me to see a guy take a swing at one of the three gigantic dudes surrounding him, all of whom looked like they'd just finished snorting cocaine in the bathroom.

"Ah, shit," the man standing on the other side of JP said. "Kevin the Cock-Block strikes again."

There was a loud sound of shattering glass and the man took off towards the bar fight, revealing Anne-Marie standing there with a worried look on her face. Beside her, Celine was chewing her lip, her eyebrows furrowed into a pained expression.

"Come on, Nellie."

JP's voice was in my ear, low and calming and direct. I swallowed, ignoring the odd way it made me shiver, and let him take my arm and lead me past the now three-on-two fight while Anne-Marie and Celine tailed us. Walking as quickly as I could to keep up with JP, none of us said anything as we left the cacophony of the bar for the relative quietness of the parking lot. It wasn't until we were all comfortably in his BMW—I ducked into the back seat with Celine before Anne-Marie could force me to take the front again—that anyone spoke.

"Well, you proved me wrong, Nellie," JP said, turning his key in the ignition.

"Huh?" I said.

His eyes met mine in the rear-view mirror, the corners crinkled. "I gave it twenty minutes before you were begging to leave, but you handled it for a whole thirty-two."

Chapter Nine
The Last Day of Summer

Two days before I had to leave for Ottawa, I accepted failure.

"It's fine, Annie," I said, my voice as heavy as the muggy late August air.

We were floating in my dad's pool while he and Brayleigh were out with some of his business partners, Anne-Marie swishing her feet back and forth in a lazy kick that just barely made her floatie turn.

"It is not *fine*," she grumbled, though I wasn't sure she was grumbling because of what I said or because of the aforementioned humidity.

"I've been picky," I said.

She shook her head, or at least attempted to. The thickness of the air seemed to make everything move more slowly. "I don't know that there is any hope for the men of the world if we cannot find one decent option to bump uglies with my most beautiful friend."

"Well, we've only checked Montreal."

She snickered. "True. Perhaps there will be a better selection in Ottawa."

I smiled, even though I didn't feel like smiling. Because I *was* fine with it.

Sort of.

Mostly.

It hadn't been the summer I'd dreamed of. In fairness, I'd never dreamed of a summer spent living with my dad while lying to my mom so I could afford to go to the university of my choice, but it also hadn't been the summer I'd expected after that whole situation became my reality.

I hadn't lost my virginity. Clearly. But after that night at Les Bleus, I'd been extra picky.

The reason for that was mostly obvious. Not that I'd admit it out loud, but I'd been scared. Celine had apologized over and over again for getting distracted by her friends as JP drove us home, even though it wasn't her fault that the man had acted the way he did. And I'd told her it was okay. That I was fine. Nothing bad had happened and she shouldn't worry about it because I wasn't going to worry about it.

And I wasn't worrying about it.

I was just being a lot more cautious, which meant I was being pickier about the people I approached.

Then there was the less-obvious reason.

Or, at least, what I thought was the less-obvious reason.

"You know, you could probably just ask him," Anne-Marie said.

I jolted, water sloshing around my shoulders as I tore my eyes away from the Marchands' deck and turned to Anne-Marie, who was looking at me with a shit-eating grin on her face. "What? Ask who?"

"Jean-Paul."

"For what?"

She looked at me over her sunglasses. "You know what."

"Oh my God," I groaned, tilting my head back. "How many times do I have to say—"

"Nellie. You like him."

My face went warm. "I do not. I never have. And, if you'll remember, *he's* not interested in that, either."

She made an exasperated and melodramatic sound. "I do not think he meant it the way you think he did."

"What else would he have meant?" I asked, bewildered. "He literally said I was like a sister. Which is *fine*, because I don't—"

"He did not," she said patiently. "He said he wouldn't let anything happen to you."

Which was half-true.

I'd followed JP and Anne-Marie inside after we dropped Celine off that night. I had to; I was not only wearing Anne-Marie's dress, but I'd left a bunch of my things in her room before we went out. But it wasn't until we were in the hallway outside their bedrooms that I forced myself to speak.

"JP?" I said quietly as he went to open his door.

"Yeah?"

"Thanks for driving us tonight," I said. "Even though we definitely didn't need it."

"Don't be too flattered. I owed Anne-Marie a favour."

I glanced at Anne-Marie, who was smirking. "For what?"

"He allowed one of his little hookups to use my bathroom when I was at Remy's one night and he *says* that is the reason my hair dryer mysteriously broke," Anne-Marie said. "I am not entirely sure she was the one using it, though."

"And yet, it doesn't matter at all, since I've now made up for it," JP said.

"Okay, well, either way," I said before Anne-Marie could say anything else. "Thanks for driving us."

"No problem," he said.

There was an awkward pause, then I cleared my throat.

"And, um, I appreciate you stepping in to help me with that guy." My voice came out in a mumble and I couldn't look at him. "So, thanks."

Even though I wasn't looking at him, I could hear the smile in his voice. "Anytime, Nellie."

I nodded brusquely. "Even though I had it handled."

"Of course you did."

"Yeah. Exactly. So I don't have to owe you a favour or anything, since I would've taken care of it anyway."

He laughed. "I see how it is. Well, since I was DDing to make up for Anne-Marie's hair dryer being broken, how about we agree this can finally make up for the time I ruined your shoes?"

I looked up, confused for a moment, then realized he was talking about the light-up shoes he'd wrecked when we were kids. "I guess so. But I don't know if it makes up for pushing me into the flower bed. I mean, it's not like that guy even tried to punch you in the face or anything."

"Oh, I wouldn't've let him do that," JP said.

"Because you would've totally kicked his ass, of course."

Surprisingly, JP shook his head. "Nah. I would've just moved out of the way. No offense, but there aren't many people I'd risk"—he gestured at his face—"all this for."

"Good to know where we stand," I said dryly.

He laughed again. "I'm kidding, Nell. I wouldn't have let anything happen to you, just like I wouldn't let anything happen to my sister."

And like, that was fine.

It was more than fine, actually. It was kind of sweet that JP thought of me like a sister. I didn't have any siblings, so I didn't know what that was like.

But even though Anne-Marie and I had this conversation multiple times since that night, she was still convinced that JP and I would be perfect together.

"Guys don't compare girls they're into to their sisters," I said to Anne-Marie for what felt like the thousandth time as she cupped her hands so she could splash some pool water on her face. "And if they do, that's something I absolutely *don't* want to be involved in."

"You are assuming men think about these things the same way women do," she said for what was also probably the thousandth time. "And they do not. Like, he was saying he cares for you as he cares for his sister. Not that he thinks of you *like* a sister."

"Those are the same thing."

"They are not." She rolled her eyes. "If anything, he was probably saying he thinks you and I should be sisters."

"I hate to break it to you, but that would still make me his sister," I said. "You know how your brother's brother is also your brother?"

She made a tutting sound. "That is not the only way it works. If you married him, we would be sisters."

"Well, I will not be doing that," I said.

"Oh, come on. I don't mind that you like him. Just tell JP you have a crush on him."

"I *don't* have a crush on him!"

"Sure, and the sky isn't blue, and this pool isn't filled with water." She giggled and splashed me. "Your face is so red. You must need more sunscreen."

"Oh, shut up," I muttered, diving under the water to get away from her.

Because of course I had a crush on him.

Of fucking *course* I did.

It was stupid. It was *ridiculous.*

Especially because I didn't want him.

Not just him. I didn't want anyone. The more I'd dated that summer, the more I'd realized that I wanted nothing to do with relationships.

Why would I? Like, sure, I knew some people who had good ones. Anne-Marie and Remy seemed pretty solid. But that was an exception, and as much as I thought the two of them were good together, there was no guarantee it would always be an exception.

Relationships were how people hurt each other. How they controlled each other. One day, you thought you were in love, and the next, you had to sit there and swallow the bitter agony of knowing you misjudged someone that fucking badly. That the amazing person you'd based your world around was making jokes about forcing you to have sex because he thought it made him sound cool.

My dad had more girlfriends than I could remember. And yet, he never seemed happy with any of them. But he also hadn't been happy when he was with my mom, even though he'd tried to get her to stay.

And my mom? She hadn't so much as flirted with anyone since the divorce—or if she had, she'd done a damn good job of hiding it—and was one of the happiest people I knew.

So I was done. I was done with relationships, at least for now. And I was honestly starting to wonder if sex would even be worth it. Anne-Marie had said I should just get losing my v-card over with because it wasn't the big deal I thought it was and I'd always thought she was a little wrong, but maybe she was wrong in a different way than I'd thought.

Maybe sex overall wasn't a big deal.

And maybe I would've believed that if it wasn't for JP.

Because I couldn't stop thinking about doing it with him and I hated it. I *hated* that stupid JP with his stupid blonde hair and big stupid blue eyes and stupid little smirk gave me that weird, warm feeling somewhere deep in my core, and I hated that I couldn't stop thinking about the way his hand had felt on my back as he stood up for me at Les Bleus. I hated that I liked him stepping in even though I *could* have taken care of myself. I hated that I'd half-wished Anne-Marie would've gone into her room and left me and JP alone in the hallway that night, and I fucking *hated* that the butterfly flutters in my heart had been crushed when he said I was like his sister.

I hated that he made me feel shy.

Because for some godforsaken reason, the idea of people *knowing* that I liked JP, someone I had absolutely no chance with because I was just his little sister's friend, was more than I could handle.

Which is why, when Anne-Marie had caught me gazing over the fence at the balcony on the back of the Marchands' house because JP was out there with his dad, I'd told her to shut up and dove under the water to end the conversation.

"I'm sorry, *chérie*," Anne-Marie said when I surfaced. "You know I am teasing, right?"

I squeezed the water out of my hair. "I know. It's fine."

"You *would* be cute with him, but Jean-Paul is a manwhore. You certainly deserve better than him for your first time."

"Annie, seriously," I said, glancing nervously at the house behind me. "Not so loud."

"I know." She held up her hands in surrender. "I am just saying."

"Well, you need to stop saying." I gestured towards the back door. "Especially here."

Because that was the other reason this summer hadn't been quite what I'd expected.

I couldn't quite explain it. Any other person in my position would've been thrilled. My dad had covered all of my school expenses. We'd gone to Ottawa together one weekend to sign the paperwork for the apartment he was renting for me and I'd almost fainted when I realized how nice it was. The second week I'd been in Montreal, he handed me a credit card connected to his account and told me to use it for anything, and that was after he'd slipped a healthy allowance into my personal bank account. I spent the summer coming and going as I pleased, lounging in the pool with Anne-Marie and going shopping and out to the clubs.

And for the first few weeks, I was certain—fucking *certain*—that my mom acted the way she did because she was bitter or something. That obviously something had happened between them, but he had my best interests at heart. That he wasn't anything like the cold, uncaring person she'd made him out to be.

And then things had just... changed.

First there was Brayleigh and her constant dislike of me. The snide little remarks and the plastic way she acted around my dad. The silver lining there was that I could see my dad getting annoyed with her, too, which meant that the next time I visited—because oh yeah, even though I'd already planned to visit as often as possible to show how grateful I was for his help, *that* expectation had been repeated enough times that it took away the shimmer of thinking he was doing all this to help me just because he was my dad—Brayleigh would probably be replaced with a new model.

But then there were the things he said about school, backhanded little comments that I wasn't sure how to take.

"It does sound prestigious," he'd said over dinner one night when I was telling him about the forensic science program I was in. "It's not law school, but it is still a huge accomplishment, *ma fille ange.*"

Another night, when I told him I was thinking of taking extra classes so I could get a double major, he'd nodded thoughtfully.

"Or you could complete your bachelor's degree more quickly," he'd said. "You would be able to start a graduate program sooner that way."

"I'm not sure about grad school yet," I'd said. "I was thinking I might do it all at once, but there's something to be said for real world experience, too."

He'd hummed dismissively. "Certainly, but you could easily apply for law school and begin a career long before you'd finish graduate studies."

"I'm not going to law school," I had said. "I don't want to be a lawyer."

"Well, things can change," he'd said, but before I could respond, Brayleigh decided he'd paid too much attention to me and started talking about some luncheon they were going to.

Then there was the way my dad seemed to think he had control of my social life. And as frustrating as it was, I *did* understand a bit of why he acted the way he did. I mean, he'd gone from being a parent on the occasional weekends and holidays to having me around full time. And the last time he'd been a full time parent, I'd been a lot younger, so the way he parented would've been completely different.

But that was no excuse for treating me like I was so… so *not* an adult.

"You will be home before eleven, then?" he'd asked one weekend when I said I was going over to Anne-Marie's to get ready to go out for the night.

"Uh… no?" I said, confused. "We won't be heading to the bar until around ten."

"Hmm." His mouth tightened. "That will not work."

"Why?" I asked.

"Because your curfew is eleven."

I laughed. He didn't.

"Dad, I'm eighteen," I said when I realized he was serious.

"So you should have plenty of experience with a curfew, then," he said.

I almost laughed again, but that definitely wouldn't have helped.

"Well, no," I said. "Mom never gave me a curfew."

I wasn't sure if it was because I brought up my mom or because I said fine, I'd just stay over at Anne-Marie's or Celine's instead of coming home, but my dad dropped the curfew thing. Well, sort of. He didn't implement a curfew, but he kept making passive-aggressive comments whenever I went out.

"Another one?" he said when I popped into his office to tell him I was going on a date a few days after that.

"Uh, yeah," I said.

"With the same boy as last time?"

I shook my head. "No, things didn't work out with him, so—"

"So it's *another* new one," he interrupted.

My spine tensed, the implication a familiar echo that sent me back to the hallways of my high school. "It's just a date, Dad. We're going for ice cream."

"*Ma fille ange*, please understand." He sat back in his chair and looked at me in a way that I think was meant to come across as mentoring but just looked condescending. "Men do not want a woman who has *dated* the entire world before them."

Heated anger rose up my chest and into my neck and cheeks. I responded to him, though I couldn't remember exactly what I said. It was something to the effect of insisting I'd only been on a few dates because I managed to stop myself from snapping and asking if that was why he kept dating women who were only a few years older than me.

Because saying that might make my dad mad enough to change his mind about helping me with school. And considering my mom had no idea what I was doing, I didn't have a backup plan if he backed out. So now it was a balancing act of living my life the way I wanted to and not letting my dad find out.

Which was why Anne-Marie needed to watch her mouth when she was talking about anything sex-related where my dad or Brayleigh might hear her.

"Alright, I am sorry," Anne-Marie said, then mimed zipping her mouth shut. "Your father still is not home, but I will say nothing more. What do you say we go out tonight, *chérie*?"

I shrugged. "If you want. But just for fun, right? Because I'm not looking for someone to hook up with anymore."

"You still could," she said. "Perhaps it will be one of those first-sight things. We can get all dressed up and find some dreamy man to show you the sexual ropes and take your mind off my brother so that when you have sex with *him*—"

I turned onto my back and kicked my legs, sending a torrent of water cascading over Anne-Marie as she cackled with laughter.

Chapter Ten
A Very Serious Dick-scussion

"There you are, Eleanor."

I nearly shit myself.

Which would have been especially unfortunate since I was just wearing the pink bikini I'd been in all day.

Luckily, I only almost crashed to the kitchen floor after jumping and skidding on a few errant drops of water that had fallen as I whirled around to see Brayleigh sitting at the kitchen table.

"I didn't know you were home," I said, gasping as adrenaline made my heart race almost painfully. "And for the last time, call me Nellie."

"Well, for the last time, drop your attitude." She stood and folded her arms. "Especially since you should thank me."

"For what?" I asked.

"For warning you that your father decided about half an hour ago to have an impromptu dinner party with his business partners and they are all in the living room, so strutting through the house in a tiny pink bikini may not go over well," she said.

I blinked.

That actually *was* something I should thank her for. My dad would have lost it if I cut through the living room dripping wet in a bikini, which I absolutely would have done because my room was right at the top of the staircase at the front of the house. This way, I could use the secondary staircase and avoid anyone seeing me.

"And you're sitting in the kitchen instead of with them because...?"

"Because I said I would let you know about this." She looked at her nails. "Since I don't want you here while we host this party. So when I saw you getting out of the pool, I thought I would wait here so I could suggest you get some clothing and then find somewhere else to be for the evening."

I rolled my eyes. "You should've picked something better. Anne-Marie and I are going out anyway."

"Good. Perhaps you can stay at the Marchands'."

"Are you going to tell my dad it was your idea for me to not come home?" I asked.

Her mouth twisted. "Why? Considering his little angel daughter has spent most of the summer tramping around on all sorts of dates, he'll still be scandalized when you don't return."

"So what do I have to gain by doing this, then?"

She opened her mouth, then glared at me as she realized there *wasn't* any real benefit to me. "Just do it, Eleanor."

"I'd rather not upset my dad," I said, feigning innocence as obviously as I could so Brayleigh knew I was faking it. "You know, seeing as he's my dad and I respect him and all."

She huffed, then rolled her eyes. "Fine. I will inform him I requested that you stay next door. Should he prefer you come home, he can call you himself."

That was better than nothing. "Fine."

"I'm glad we're in agreement." She started towards the living room, then stopped when she was nearly out of the kitchen. "Oh, and I suggest you get out of here in the next five minutes, since your father is planning on giving them a tour of the house as soon as I return and let him know I've told you we have guests."

Well, fuck.

I moved as fast as I could. I didn't bother changing out of my bikini, just threw a long t-shirt on over top before collecting my makeup, purse, and a hairbrush. Even still, my dad's voice was floating up the stairs when I cracked my door open to leave, so I scurried down the hall and down the back stairs again.

When I got to the Marchands', I let myself in without knocking since Anne-Marie said her parents were out. But I had told Anne-Marie I was going to take a shower before coming over, so she clearly wasn't expecting me and jumped in surprise when I got up to her room.

"Brayleigh was being a—oh." I pressed my lips closed as I realized her phone was pressed to her ear, then grimaced as I realized she was wrapped in a towel and had wet hair. "*Sorry.*"

Something wicked sparkled in her eyes and she put a finger to her lips.

"I am *fine*, Remy," she said haughtily. "Nellie has just arrived, so you have lost your chance completely. I am going out with her tonight and that is final." She waited for a moment, then huffed loudly. "*Arrête d'essayer de me contrôler.* Don't you dare come over tonight."

With that, she hung up.

"Are you okay?" I asked, frowning.

"Oh, yes." She put her phone down, a smile spreading across her lips. "Remy and I are just playing our little game."

"What little—oh." My face burned. "Your jealousy sex game."

"Yes. I expect he'll turn up once we return tonight."

"Ah." I bit my lip. "Okay."

Anne-Marie frowned. "What is wrong, *chérie?*"

"Nothing. Brayleigh was being a bitch and she told my dad I was going to be here tonight while they host a dinner party. But don't worry about it. I'm sure I can sneak in."

She started shaking her head before I finished speaking. "You can absolutely stay, Nellie. I will tell Remy he cannot come over for real. Or…" She tapped a finger to her chin. "I mean, there is the guest room."

"I don't mind sleeping in the guest room," I said.

She shook her head. "No, that will make it too obvious to my parents that Remy is over. You can stay here while Remy and I mess up the guest room. Unless you find some sexy man to go home with instead."

"I'm not going home with anyone tonight."

"Not with that attitude."

I rolled my eyes. "Whatever. Can I use your shower? And your shampoo? I didn't even grab mine."

She got a spare towel for me, then grabbed her hair dryer since she knew I would take my time in the shower. Long, hot showers were a guilty pleasure of mine. I'd always tried to be quick, but as soon as the stream of hot water hit me, the noise of it filling my ears and the sensation of it covering my body, it was like my brain turned off for a bit.

And she knew that, mainly because of the amount of times that summer I'd told her I would come over after taking a shower and show up an hour and a half or two hours later. But I was a guest at the Marchands', so even though I still took a while, I figured it would be rude to take as long as I usually did.

But I was wrong.

"Hey, are you done with the hair dryer?" I asked, casually opening the bathroom door after wrapping myself in a towel. "Or do you—oh!"

My eyes went wide as Anne-Marie whirled around. Her face was red, though it probably had less to do with being embarrassed and more to do with the fact that Remy was standing in front of her, his eyes wide as he belatedly shielded the very obvious bulge in the front of his unzipped pants. Anne-Marie had put on clothes while I was in the shower, but the form-fitting dress she was wearing was hiked up high enough that I could see the crotch of her red panties. She burst out laughing and tugged it down.

"Oops," she gasped. "Sorry, Nellie. I thought you would be longer. Um, would you... Could you maybe give me and Remy a few minutes to finish our, um, very serious discussion?"

"More like dick-scussion," I muttered. "Jesus Christ, Annie."

I'd left my things on her bed before getting in the shower, but Anne-Marie had obviously moved them once Remy arrived. Face burning as I clutched the front of the towel to my chest, I scrambled around her room, grabbing my makeup bag off the dresser and snatching up the hair dryer she'd set next to it.

"We'll be quick," Anne-Marie promised as I left the room.

"No, we won't," Remy said, but by then the door had closed. There was the muffled sound of Anne-Marie giggling again, though it turned into a yelp followed by a breathy gasp.

"Oh, *Remy*," she said.

I made a disgusted face.

Then I looked down at my hands.

Then, very slowly, I realized I'd grabbed three things.

Anne-Marie's hair dryer.

My makeup bag.

And my hairbrush.

However, I had no pants—not that I'd been wearing any when I arrived—and I hadn't grabbed any of Anne-Marie's dresses. Nor had I grabbed the t-shirt I'd worn over my bikini, and I was belatedly realizing that I hadn't even grabbed a pair of panties or a bra before I left my house.

I mean, not that the bra was super necessary. Despite my boobs being a little too big to get away with not wearing a bra normally, the dresses Anne-Marie lent me were tight enough on me that I didn't need one.

But still. I didn't even have my fucking *bikini*.

The thing was, if the Marchands lived in a normal house, it would've been fine. Not *fine*, but there would have been a bathroom nearby that I could duck into and sit in until Anne-Marie and Remy were done fucking.

But the Marchands did not live in a normal house. They lived in a house where all the bedrooms apparently had ensuites, so there was no need to have a main bathroom down that hallway. And yes, they had plenty of other bathrooms—there were three on the main level and probably the same amount on the lowest level—but getting to any of them would require marching through the house clad only in a towel.

Twice.

Because I *also* hadn't grabbed my phone so I could message Anne-Marie about my predicament.

I almost turned around to knock on Anne-Marie's door and tell her and Remy to keep it in their pants for five seconds so I could get dressed, but as I did, Anne-Marie moaned.

And I mean *moaned*. It was loud enough that I recoiled, my face turning red at the absolute depravity of the sound coming from my best friend's bedroom. And then, because the situation just had to get worse, that was also the moment JP entered the hallway.

JP, who was wearing those fucking *jeans* and a tight-but-not-too-tight t-shirt that showed off his biceps.

JP, with his sparkling blue eyes and thick blonde hair and wide, mischievous smile.

JP, who had a concerned but amused look on his face as his sister let out another loud squeal while I stood in the hallway with a hairdryer clutched to my chest.

"Uh... hey, Nellie," he said.

"Hi," I squeaked.

"What're you—"

"Remy's over."

He rolled his eyes. "Of course. I'm surprised she didn't call him the moment Mom and Dad left. But on the bright side, it's been a while since he's been over, so they'll probably be done in, like, five minutes."

"Oh, good."

There was an extended pause.

"D'you want to get ready in my room?" he asked.

No, I thought. No, no, no, no fucking way, the absolute last thing I wanted to do was end up in JP's room with only a towel around me so he could laugh at me in a way that hurt way more than I wanted to admit and—

Anne-Marie let out another depraved-sounding moan.

Then again, there was no reason I couldn't just lock myself in his bathroom until Anne-Marie stopped making those fucking noise.

"Yes, please," I said.

JP smirked, then jerked his head towards the door next to his sister's. "Come here, then."

Chapter Eleven
Legendary

I HAD BEEN IN JP's room a few times before.

Usually to do something stupid, like hiding plastic tarantulas in his sock drawer or painting all his pens and pencils with nail polish so when he went to do his homework, nothing would write.

But after Anne-Marie and I snuck into his bathroom and glued his deodorant, body wash, and shampoo containers shut, he complained to his parents, who let him put a lock on his door so we'd stop playing pranks on him. Which was fair, since he was a teenager and didn't want to deal with two bratty kids touching all his stuff.

Though, it didn't really end up mattering. My parents announced they were getting divorced not too long after that and I moved away.

But I'd only ever been in his room as a kid, and as I was belatedly remembering, it hadn't been *this* room.

"What's wrong?" JP asked as I took a few steps in before freezing.

The room was smaller than I'd expected. Like, *way* smaller than Anne-Marie's room. There was a desk near the window and a dresser with a mirror attached, a queen-size bed in the middle of the room, and a wardrobe closet on the far wall... but that was it.

"Where's your bathroom?" I asked.

"Downstairs," he said. "I traded rooms with Marc-Andre when I started university so he could have the room with the ensuite, since I was living in residence."

"Oh," I said, my voice high-pitched as I realized that yeah, this *hadn't* been the room we'd tried to rig with confetti on the ceiling fan, since it didn't even have a ceiling fan. "That must be inconvenient for you."

He shrugged. "This room was part of the other bedroom originally—my old bedroom—but when we moved in, my parents renovated to add a nursery since Marc-Andre was still a baby," he said. "I think they intended to turn the ensuite in the other room into a Jack and Jill type one, but never got around to it since it would require renovating the entire thing. And it seems pointless now since I'm only here over the summers."

"Right," I said.

He smirked. "Don't worry. I'll turn around so you can change. And I won't even face the mirror or anything."

"How chivalrous," I said dryly. "But I don't have my clothes."

He stared at me, then shook his head and laughed. "Shit. She really left you hanging." He walked over to the wardrobe and reached in. "Here. You can borrow my robe. It's a little more... *secure* than a towel."

It was thoughtful, even though the robe was far too large for me and smelled like his cologne, which was definitely a bad thing because his cologne smelled *amazing*. He turned away, facing the back wall of his room while I shrugged it on and secured the robe tie as tight as I could.

And at that point, I could've left his room.

I was covered. There were other bathrooms I could go to. JP had said his parents weren't home, so it wasn't like anyone would see me.

But for some reason, none of those things came to mind.

"Is it okay if I dry my hair in here?" I asked.

"Yeah, of course," JP said. "Do you want me to go or...?"

I shook my head. "It's fine."

He shrugged, then showed me where the plug-in next to his dresser was before settling on his bed with a book. I dried my hair, which didn't take overly long—my hair wasn't especially thick and Anne-Marie's replacement hair dryer was apparently *very* high end—and once I was done, I unplugged it and wrapped the cord up.

"Well, thanks," I said.

JP looked up from his book. "What?"

"For letting me use your room." I gestured at the door. "I'm gonna go now."

"Are you?" he asked, amused.

My face started getting warm. "Uh... yes? They should be done, shouldn't—"

And then a banging sound started on the wall.

"I was joking about the five minutes," JP said.

"Clearly," I muttered.

He grinned. "You didn't know that?"

"I did," I said. "I was just trying to get out of your hair."

"Hmm, right," he said, unconvinced. "Haven't you had sex before, Nellie?"

Thank God JP's robe swallowed me the way it did, because I was pretty sure my entire body turned red.

And I don't know why I didn't say yes. I don't know *why* I couldn't just admit that yeah, I was a virgin, and he'd been one once too, which meant there was a time when he didn't know how long sex was supposed to take, so he could shut up and stop making fun of me.

That was a lie. I did know why I didn't say yes, and it was because the thought of JP laughing at me was almost painful. Like admitting I was a virgin was admitting to failure. Which it kind of was, I guess. It was a failed relationship and a summer full of failed attempts to meet someone who would have sex with me. And maybe that meant there was something wrong with me, or that no one wanted me, or—

It didn't matter.

What mattered was that I couldn't tell JP I was a virgin.

But I also couldn't bring myself to lie to him.

"That's literally none of your business," I said.

He held up a hand defensively. "Of course. Just asking."

I turned back around, opening the makeup bag I'd put on his dresser and pretending I couldn't see him looking at me in the mirror. After a moment, he turned back to his book and I started doing my makeup.

Well, I tried to, anyway.

"What's the trouble?" JP asked a few minutes later after I took out a makeup wipe and cleaned my face off far more aggressively than was necessary before zipping my bag shut in frustration.

"Sleeves," I grunted.

"Huh?"

"The sleeves." I held up my arm, batting the excess fabric away to prove my point. "They're too big for me."

"Probably because I buy things that fit me, not random girls who end up camping out in my room to avoid my sister."

"It's fine. They should be done soon, right?"

Anne-Marie picked that moment to moan again and JP stifled another laugh. "Uh... maybe."

I groaned in frustration, walking over to the bed and sitting on the edge. "Jesus. Do you have to listen to them every single time?"

JP shrugged. "They tend to keep it quieter when my parents are home, but I usually put headphones on."

"Sorry. You can if you want."

"It's fine. The hair dryer drowned it out for a bit. And now we can suffer awkwardly together."

I laughed in spite of myself, then did exactly as JP said and suffered awkwardly.

At least JP had his book. All I could do was stare at an empty patch of nothing on his bedroom floor because there wasn't anything for me to look at. Apparently JP wasn't the kind of person who had random bobby pins and tubes of mascara and clothes tags discarded all over the place.

Or the Marchands had a cleaner, which was probably more likely. My dad did too, but I'd been refusing to let them clean my room while I was there over the summer, much to his chagrin.

Regardless, the fact that I had nothing to do and nothing to look at was a problem. Mainly because I didn't have nothing to listen to. I had *plenty* to listen to, because being a gossipy loudmouth apparently extended into Anne-Marie's bedroom activities too. Cry after muffled cry came through the wall between her room and JP's and... well.

I mean, it was hard not to wonder what was making her make those noises.

It was hard not to imagine what they were doing.

And it was very, very, *very* difficult to stop my body from reacting to those mental images.

I swallowed hard, using my thumb to pick at my nails beneath the swaths of sleeve fabric covering my hands. Everything about this felt weird. Listening to my best friend have what seemed to be very satisfying sex was weird, especially since I... I just...

I mean, the noises were just...

It wasn't like I *liked* the noises she was making.

But apparently, my body did.

So yeah. Hearing the sounds they made was weird. Getting turned on by said sounds was super weird. Picturing it was super *fucking* weird.

But what made everything extra super fucking weird was being in the room with someone I found horrendously attractive. And that was probably why I was reacting the way I was, because yeah, a semi-disgusted part of me wondered exactly what Remy was doing to make Anne-Marie make those noises... but a bigger part of me was wondering if JP could make someone make noises like that.

If JP could make *me* make noises like that.

And wondering that while wrapped in nothing but his robe, enveloped in the scent of his shampoo or his body wash or maybe his cologne, my breasts pressed into the plush fabric and my pussy starting to get wet and—

Oh, fuck.

I was going to leave a wet spot on his fucking robe.

As casually as I could, I stood from the edge of the bed, hoping he'd believe I'd shifted to start pacing in restless impatience. Another loud noise filtered through the wall, but this time it wasn't Anne-Marie.

That was Remy, and he was saying something in French that I couldn't quite make out, and then he...

Oh God.

He fucking *whimpered.*

"Jeez," JP said with a chuckle. "They're really into it this time. You catching them must have done something for them."

"Great," I said, my tone flat, then sighed. "Doesn't it bug you?"

"What?" JP asked. "The sound?"

"Well and... I mean, I find it weird and she's just my friend. You're her brother."

From the corner of my eye, I saw JP shrug. "Yeah, but it's just sex. It's not like I'm into hearing them fuck or something, but it's not a big deal."

I swallowed hard and shifted, embarrassed of the slickness between my thighs. "Right. Of course."

He glanced up at me. "Why? Do you have some kind of hang-up about sex?"

"No," I said.

"You're not waiting for marriage or something?"

I glared. Not at him, because that would have required me to look at him and I didn't think I could handle actually putting my eyes on him. Instead, I glared at the clean floor of his bedroom. "Why would you even think that?"

"Well, there's all the blushing and the questions..."

"I'm just making conversation," I said as convincingly as I could, which was probably not very convincingly at all. "But if you'd rather sit here and awkwardly listen, fine."

And then for some reason, I felt like I needed to punctuate that sentence by plopping myself back onto the edge of his bed, folding my arms and crossing one leg over the other. JP chuckled but didn't respond. Instead, I sat there stubbornly, thankful that at least JP's robe was thick enough that he wouldn't be able to see my nipples pressing into it. And once Anne-Marie was done, I could keep his robe on while I went back to her room, then I could lock myself in the bathroom and make sure I hadn't left any wet spots on the robe or let them dry if I had, and—

"Who was your first time with, then?" JP asked.

Startled, I stuttered for a moment. "That's... That's not your business either."

"Ah, come on. Tell me." He closed his book and shifted on the bed, rolling onto his side and propping himself up on his elbow. "It wasn't your high school boyfriend. I know that much."

My mouth dropped open and I whirled around. "What? How... how do you know that?"

He almost looked sympathetic. Almost. He was too busy holding in a laugh to look actually sympathetic. "Don't ever tell Anne-Marie anything you wouldn't put on a billboard beside the highway."

I was too shocked to even be upset. "And she told you... what did she tell you?"

Something about my voice made JP pause. "Just that you broke up with him because he was an asshole. Enough of one that she'd like to run him down with her car."

I let out a soft snort. "Well, that's accurate."

"What did he do?"

I tried to laugh, mostly because there was enough concern hidden beneath the curiosity in JP's voice that I didn't know how to handle it. "Why do you want to know? Are you gonna go all 'protective big brother' on me again?"

He paused again, though that time, it seemed to be because he was bewildered. "What do you mean, big brother?"

I shrugged, redness creeping up my cheeks as I looked away from him again. "You know. Like at the bar."

He laughed. "Jeez, Nellie. I dunno what kind of relationship you think Anne-Marie and I have, but if there had been some creep hitting on her, I would've gone with the 'leave my sister alone' approach over the 'pretending to be your boyfriend' thing."

He...

What?

I blinked, staring at his bedroom floor.

If he thought of me like a sister, he would've...

Oh my God.

And maybe I was in shock. Or maybe the realization that maybe JP *didn't* see me as a sister scrambled my brain. Maybe he asked me again what Adrian had done to me.

Whatever it was, the next thing I knew, I was telling JP what happened.

Not all of it, at least not in specifics. I didn't want to repeat the exact things Adrian had said to his friends about me.

But I did tell JP that while I didn't go out of my way to tell other people what Adrian had said, I wasn't going to lie about it, especially when other girls had a right to know when a guy says something like that.

That told JP enough. The blue of his eyes seemed to darken, enough that I knew he didn't need the specifics to understand what I meant and that even before he spoke, he agreed with me.

And I told him I had screenshots of what Adrian had said. And that when it got back to Adrian that people knew what he said, he hadn't given them the same song and dance about it just being guy talk.

No, instead he'd told everyone that the screenshots were fake.

That the story I was telling was fake.

That I'd come up with this whole fabricated tale myself after he broke up with me because he'd found out I had not only lied about being a virgin, but that I didn't even know who I'd lost my virginity to.

"What do you mean, you don't know?" JP asked.

I glared at him. "I didn't say I don't know. I said *he* said I don't know."

JP held up his hand. "Right. But how—"

"Because apparently that's what happens when you go to an out-of-town volleyball tournament and a bunch of teams are all staying in the same hotel," I said. "And since there happens to be a guys' tournament happening that same weekend, everyone starts partying together at the hotel on the last night. And of course, the most logical explanation for you leaving the party early isn't that you twisted your knee during the final set of the gold medal game. It's that a couple of guys from Kingston convinced you to go back to their room, one thing led to another, and suddenly you were in the middle of an orgy with a bunch of high school volleyball players and couldn't remember who'd gone first."

"And people believed that?"

"Well, I couldn't prove I was back in my room by myself sleeping," I said. "And apparently a friend of a friend of a guy who was involved met Adrian at U of T and told him about it, so suddenly I was a slut trying to ruin his reputation so I could keep mine intact. Which meant hardly anyone wanted to stay friends with me."

And fucking *no one* had wanted to date me, but I kept that to myself.

JP shook his head. "People love a sensationalized story. I'm sorry, Nell. For what it's worth, I would've still been your friend."

I laughed, mostly because the idea that JP would be friends with me if we'd gone to high school together made my stomach feel oddly warm and fuzzy. "You wouldn't have thought I was some huge slut who couldn't even tell you my body count because it was so high after my first time?"

He looked at me carefully, his head tilted. "You know it's okay to enjoy sex, right?"

"I never said it wasn't."

"Like, yeah, it was horrible for him to do that, but even if it was true, it wouldn't make you a slut. And honestly, it *would* have been a great first time story."

I stared at him, horrified. "What?"

The corner of JP's mouth tugged up into a smile that was part wicked, part impressed. "Come on. Losing your v-card during an orgy? *That's* fucking legendary." He paused, then snickered. "And legendary fucking too, I guess."

"So you'd be impressed," I said. "If that was how I'd lost my virginity."

"If that was how you wanted to do it? Hell yeah, I'd be impressed." He thought for a moment. "I guess I understand it. It seemed like a way bigger deal in high school. But there's nothing wrong with sleeping around, Nellie."

I didn't know what to say. Who would? After losing friends and having my classmates and even my teachers tell me I was a slut for months, JP was sitting there telling me that even if the rumour had been true, he wouldn't have thought I was a slut, and that he would've been *impressed*?

It was unsettling and confusing in the best and worst way.

"But that still doesn't answer my question," he said.

"What question?" I asked.

"What your first time was like," he said. "Now I know it wasn't an orgy. So was it super sweet and romantic? Something out of a fairytale?"

"Why does it even matter?" I asked.

"Because." A second later, his foot nudged my back and I nearly fell off the bed. Not because he nudged me hard, but the shock of feeling someone touch me paired with the way that my entire body was tingling was almost unsettling. "You keep saying you're not a virgin, but the only proof you've presented was a situation about how people *said* you weren't a virgin."

I hadn't actually said that I wasn't a virgin, but I wasn't going to hand that little technicality to him. "Don't lawyer me."

He burst out laughing. "*Lawyer* you?"

"Yeah. You're trying to be all lawyerly about things and interrogate me. I'm not falling for it." I clenched my legs, tightening them beneath his robe. "And you're not very good at it, either."

He kept snickering. "I'm not an actual lawyer yet, so don't worry. But—"

"What was your first time like then?" I asked, not sure if I was trying to deflect him or throw him off. Because it wasn't because I wanted to know.

Definitely not.

But either way, it didn't work.

"Super shitty," he said. "I lasted about ten seconds and she cried after."

"Oh."

He shrugged. "I got better at it."

I pressed my lips together in amusement. "Good to know."

"Is it?"

"What?"

"Good to know?"

I rolled my eyes. "It's just an expression."

"Sure." He nudged me with his foot again. "Was yours any better than that?"

"I mean, it is what it is."

"That's not an answer, Nell."

Annoyed, I glared at his floor again. "Why do you want to know so bad?"

The mattress moved as he shifted on the bed. "Well, since you're apparently shit at taking hints, I'm trying to figure out if I can hit on you or not."

It was a good thing I was facing away from him.

There would've been no way for me to recover any dignity if JP had seen the way my eyes went wide and my lips parted. It wasn't possible for my face to get any redder than it was, so at least I wasn't blushing, but...

Fuck.

He wanted to know...

Oh my God.

Even after I told him about the rumours, he...

Oh my *God*.

He had to be joking.

"You're hitting on me?" I asked.

"No," he said.

My throat flexed as I swallowed back a lump that was definitely relief and not at all embarrassment that I'd actually thought he was hitting on me. There was an awkward moment of silence before JP chuckled.

"I *want* to hit on you," he continued. "I mean, look at you, Nellie. You're hot as fuck and contrary to popular belief, I *am* only human. But I don't want to make it weird, especially when you're sitting in my bedroom wearing only a robe."

Oh. So he wasn't hitting on me.

He just... wanted to hit on me.

He wanted...

Oh my God.

He called me hot.

Hot as *fuck*, even.

I was sitting.

In JP's bedroom.

Wearing his robe.

And he'd just called me hot and now I had to decide what the fuck to do because he said he wanted to hit on me and—

Oh. My. *God*.

His words hung in the silence between us until they were knocked down by a series of high-pitched moans reverberating through the wall. JP cleared his throat and I shattered the moment, jumping at the unexpected sound. The mattress moved again as he shifted back, giving me space.

"Obviously it would be weird," he said. "I'm sorry, Nell. Look, you can pretend you're not a virgin all you want, but I don't want to make you uncomfortable. If you want to hang out in here until they're done, I can go downstairs and—"

And maybe if Anne-Marie hadn't been moaning the way she was.

Maybe if I wasn't naked under that robe.

Maybe if my heart hadn't been racing the way it was.

Maybe, just fucking *maybe*, if it hadn't been JP in that room with me, I would've said something different.

I would've done something different.

But my head felt dizzy and I was panicking because he was about to leave and I didn't *want* him to leave because of course I had a crush on JP and this could be...

This could be it.

So before it was over, before he could get off the bed, before I could so much as think it through, I made my decision.

"What is it going to take for you to stop thinking I'm a virgin?" I asked.

"Nellie, you—"

"Will you believe it if I have sex with you?"

"—shouldn't be... wait. What?"

I stood up, turning around to finally look at him, hoping the look on my face was fierce and determined instead of uncertain or uncomfortable.

Because after all, how hard could it be? I knew what sex was. I was on the pill; my mom had taken me to get a prescription for it when I was sixteen, even though I'd told her I wasn't having sex. Adrian and I had fooled around, so I knew the basics. I could bullshit my way through the rest.

And if I did it now, with JP... I mean, at least I was sort of getting what I wanted. JP wasn't some meaningless stranger. He wasn't going to think I was a slut if I slept with him.

So he...

He was the right choice.

"I asked if you'd believe it if I have sex with you," I repeated, then undid the belt of the robe and shrugged the blanket of soft fabric off my shoulders.

Chapter Twelve
Liar

ANNE-MARIE SAID HER FIRST time sucked.

JP said his first time sucked.

The general sentiment I'd always heard was that it just... sucked. That at best, it was weird and awkward or didn't last anywhere near as long as it needed to. At worst, it was painful and regretful. I'd heard some people say they cried—both men and women, and both during and after—and others who were so unaware of what they were supposed to be doing that they thought something was wrong with them.

In fairness, I was also worried that there was something wrong with me. But that was only because it didn't suck.

At all.

Well, not like that, anyway.

JP's robe floated off my body and onto the floor, pooling at my feet. Standing in front of him, fully naked and knowing he could see just how turned on I was, it took everything in my power not to tremble.

Not that he would have noticed if I did.

My heart was beating hard enough that JP might have been able to see my pulse through my skin, but his eyes were glued to my breasts, his mouth hanging open and his bright blue eyes round. JP was the kind of person who seemed to embody nonchalant coolness with a natural ease, so seeing his expression of shock and the hint of pink on his tanned face was new to me.

And somehow, seeing him look flustered like that...

It did *something* to me.

Something good.

"Holy shit," he finally breathed. "Right... right now?"

"If you think you can handle it." The words came out confident and sassy in a way that felt foreign and phenomenal at the same time. "Were you joking about hitting on me?"

"No," he said quickly. "No, not at all. I just... *wow*, Nellie."

His eyes raked over my body, taking in every inch of me all at once. His gaze traced my tan lines, his curiosity almost a physical sensation as he stared at the glistening skin between my thighs, probably wondering if he was seeing things or if I really was that wet.

"Are you sure?" he asked.

"Positive," I said, and was almost surprised to realize that it was completely true.

"Oh, jeez," JP whispered, then moved from his side to his back and beckoned towards me. "Come here, then."

He took off his t-shirt as I got onto the bed, chucking it to the side. I moved towards him, going immediately to the button of his jeans, but a gentle hand clasped around my wrist. I glanced up to see JP looking at me. Without a word, he let go of my arm, then moved his hand to my neck and guided me in to kiss him.

And oh, *God*.

I never knew a kiss could do to me what his did. If I'd thought every nerve in my body was heightened before, it was nothing to the way desire raced through my veins, coursing through my body and straight to the slick wetness between my legs. I took half a moment to unbutton his jeans, then abandoned them and let a hand rest on his chest as he pulled me closer and closer to him.

When my breasts touched his chest, I shivered. It was intimate in a way that shouldn't have felt so familiar. I had no choice but to crawl onto his lap, straddling his hips as we kissed. As soon as I was settled, JP's tongue slipped past my lips and flicked against mine. I gasped and felt him smile, his arms going around me and holding me tight before he let his hands skim along my back.

Another shiver ran through me as he trailed his fingertips along my spine, and another as those same fingertips traced along my ribs and up to my breast. He slipped his hand between us, cupping my breast before squeezing, then pinched my nipple between his thumb and forefinger to draw a moan from me.

"Quietly," he murmured against my mouth. "Unless you want my sister to know you're in here fucking me."

Maybe him pointing that out should have made me feel guilty, but all it did was send a wave of excitement over me, and when he rolled my nipple between his fingers again, I muffled my gasp with his mouth.

The denim of his jeans was rough on my pussy. I knew the wetness between my legs had to be staining them, but I doubted JP minded if the way his cock was bulging against me was any indication. It wasn't an unfamiliar sensation—I'd sat like this on Adrian's lap a few times, feeling his erection beneath me as we kissed on the couch in my mom's basement—but I'd never felt it like *this*, where my slit wasn't shielded by the fabric of my own jeans and panties and was instead pressed bare against his pants.

I wanted more.

I wanted it inside me. I wanted to know what it would feel like stretching me wide open and pushing in and out of me, but JP didn't seem to be in a rush to get there. He kept caressing my tits, rubbing his thumb across my nipple until I squirmed in his lap.

He dipped his head down, shifting just enough that he could press his face against my chest. I swallowed hard, then had to bite my lip when his mouth found my nipple. He ran the tip of his tongue around it, then sucked it into his mouth before grazing his teeth against the nub.

And that...

Fuck.

JP let out a soft chuckle as I squeaked, then nearly slapped myself in the face as I clapped a hand over my mouth.

"You like that?" he asked, then nibbled at the sensitive skin again.

"Yes," I hissed.

He groaned, his hands running down my sides and gripping my hips as he carefully tugged at my nipple with his teeth.

My body was on fire. I couldn't stop myself from squirming against his erection, trying to get some relief from the insistent need for friction. The desperation must have been obvious because JP's grip on my hips loosened and he slipped his hands behind me, grabbing my ass and moaning against me as he dug his fingers into it. He squeezed, then held me down, grinding my body harder against his bulge.

"You want this?" he asked.

"Yes," I whimpered.

"Better make it quick," he said, his lips brushing against my breast as he spoke. "Wouldn't want Anne-Marie to finish up and wonder where you are."

I gritted my teeth together. "Stop teasing me, then."

He pressed a kiss between my cleavage, then looked up with a sparkle in his eyes and a smirk on his lips. "But it's so fun to watch you blush."

I glared at him, but before he could laugh at me again, I leaned in and kissed him. A puff of air brushed against my mouth before he kissed me back. Once he had, I pulled away, moving backwards until he was forced to let go of my ass. Without looking up at him, I reached for the waistband of his jeans again, finishing the job I'd started and unzipping his pants before tugging them down.

His hands joined mine, helping me guide his pants down at the same time as his boxers, unceremoniously revealing his swollen cock. I tried not to stare, but that was futile. I'd seen a dick before, but it obviously wasn't the same as JP's. His was...

I mean, in hindsight, it probably wasn't *that* much bigger than Adrian's. It was a decent size, that much was true, and it definitely *seemed* bigger than the one I had experience with.

But that might have been because I knew where it was about to go.

Not that I was nervous. I wasn't.

Not even a little.

"Nellie," JP said.

I looked up at him. His eyes were heavy with desire as they met mine.

"Are you on the pill?" he asked.

I nodded.

His throat flexed as he swallowed. "Are you cool if we... uh..."

I shouldn't have been cool without him using a condom. I knew that. He wasn't a virgin—if Anne-Marie was to be believed, he'd been with a new girl every month since he'd turned eighteen. And after everything, after the rumours and the hell that my life had been for the last semester of high school, I should've said he needed one. I'm sure he wouldn't have minded one bit if I said that. He probably had a stack of them in his nightstand drawer, just a few feet away from where we were sitting.

But something inside me seemed to inherently trust JP because I nodded anyway.

He made a soft noise of appreciation, reaching forward and caressing my cheek. "You wanna be on top? I'm *really* liking having your tits in my face."

I also liked having my tits in his face, so I nodded for a third time and climbed back onto his lap, hoping he couldn't tell that I was trembling or that if he could, that he thought I was quivering with excitement or something. He adjusted himself, leaning back against the headboard as I straddled his hips, and I tried to cover a surprised jolt as the tip of his cock brushed my wet folds. My breath came in short gasps that I tried to play it off as excitement, heat rising up my cheeks as I reached down and wrapped my fingers around the hot, smooth skin of his shaft so I could position him at my entrance. He pressed a kiss against my shoulder, his breath warm on my skin.

This was really happening.

I was really doing this.

JP didn't know I was a virgin, so there was no moment of him checking to make sure I was ready or if I'd changed my mind. There was no moment where he slid inside me, pausing so I could adjust to his size as he penetrated me for the first time. No comforting hand stroked my hair. No kiss urged me to relax. No soft words talked me through what to do or urged me to take it slowly or carefully.

Instead, I bit my lip, took a quiet breath, then plunged him inside me in one single, swift movement.

And then a high-pitched yelp squeaked out of my throat as I scrunched my eyes shut.

"What the... Nellie?" JP gasped.

Fuck.

I couldn't move.

It didn't *hurt*, per se. But it felt *weird* and I couldn't make myself sit back up. There was a feeling of pressure, a stretching sensation and a foreign presence that I wasn't entirely sure I liked. Everything seemed quiet except my heart, which pounded in my ears as the rest of me panicked and tried to figure out what to do after every thought had been shoved out of my brain. Swallowing hard, I took a shallow breath to calm myself, but a soft whimper slipped out despite my desperate attempt to keep quiet.

"You fucking liar," JP said. His words might have sounded unkind, but his tone wasn't. It was almost amused, almost sad, almost impressed. "You are a virgin, aren't you?"

"Technically I never said I wasn't," I whispered.

"Shit. Oh, shit," he swore. His hands went to my hips, then to my lower back, a soothing weight against my spine. He held me still with one hand while the other moved up to my face, cupping my cheek. "Are you okay?"

I nodded.

"Liar," he said again.

My throat felt dry. "Maybe a little."

"Why didn't you tell me?"

If he felt the way my face burned beneath his touch, he didn't say anything. "I didn't want you to laugh at me."

"Oh, babe," he said, a soft chuckle making his cock jostle inside me, and I tried not to wince. "I wish you would've. I wouldn't have—"

"You wouldn't have fucked me," I said. "No one would do it with me before because they all thought I was a slut and you wouldn't have if you knew I was a virgin and I couldn't even pick some random person so I could just do it because I..." My voice cracked and I tried not to wince. "I wanted to. I've wanted to for ages. But it's like he wrecked that for me because all I could think about was that I needed to know their name." There was a lump in my throat and I swallowed hard. "I shouldn't have... I mean, it was wrong for me to... I'm sorry."

There was a heavy beat of silence, but a moment later, JP's thumb stroked my cheek.

"Nell, I still would've fucked you if you wanted me to." He moved his hand to my forehead, brushing my hair back. "Just maybe not so... suddenly."

His tone was as tender as his touch. After a moment, I pried my eyes open and forced myself to look at him. JP was looking back, concern on his face.

"Are you alright?" he asked.

I considered the question, focusing my attention on what was happening between my legs. Other than the way his cock had twitched when he chuckled, neither of us had moved, and sitting motionless seemed to have made things relax a little. There wasn't as much discomfort or pressure. Now it was just unfamiliar.

Unfamiliar and...

And kind of nice.

"I think so," I whispered.

Surprisingly, he pressed his mouth to mine and pulled me in, holding me still against his chest. My heart had been racing erratically, but it evened out as he kissed me. "Do you want to stop?"

"Do you?" I asked.

He laughed. "Babe, we'll stop if you want to. No hard feelings and no problems, ever. But if you don't, I'm *definitely* still into this."

"You're not mad?" I hated that my voice shook, but it did. "Or not mad enough to want to stop, at least?"

Another soft laugh. "I'm not mad. But if you don't want to keep going, we're stopping."

His face was still close to mine, so when I spoke, my lips brushed against his. "I want to keep going."

"You want to stay like this or do you want me to take over?"

I considered things for a moment, then shifted my hips experimentally. JP groaned, the hand he had on my back pressing down as he shuddered.

"Like this," I said. "For a bit anyway. If I... I mean... you can tell me if I suck at it."

"You'll be fine," he breathed. "Just..." He held me still again, looking up at me with a solemnness in his eyes that was almost unrecognizable. "I need you to promise me you're on the pill."

"I am," I said. "I swear. I... I promise."

"Okay," he said. "I believe you."

Then he kissed me, moved his hands to my hips, and slowly, carefully, began guiding me to ride his cock.

And oh, God.

That feeling of being stretched around him had felt weird at first, but apparently we'd sat there long enough for it to start feeling right. And the sensation of being *full* was satisfying in a way I'd never thought it could be.

And maybe it was because JP guided me to almost grind against him rather than bounce on top of him, so his pelvis brushed against my clit each time I moved. Maybe it was just getting used to it, my pussy accepting that I'd impaled myself on his rigid erection and that it was *supposed* to be good, that I was *supposed* to like it.

Whatever it was, I suddenly couldn't get enough.

JP groaned as it became clear that I liked what was happening. As I found a rhythm that made pleasure radiate from my core and clit all the way through my body, one of his hands slid around me, cupping my ass again, as the other moved up to my breasts. He gripped one gently, cupping it from underneath so he could lift it slightly as he brought his mouth down to my nipple and sank his teeth in again.

And *fuck*.

That shouldn't have felt so good, but it drew another moan from my lips, forgetting I was supposed to be quiet until the dull pounding of a bed frame against the other side of the wall reminded me that my best friend was in the next room with her boyfriend while I fucked her brother. I bit my lip, stifling the noise as best I could, and rolled my hips faster.

And then faster.

And then a feeling of warmth started to spread through my core and I realized that my first time wasn't just going to not suck.

It was going to be *good*.

I'd had orgasms before, but apparently, an orgasm felt different when there was a cock inside you. A prickling sensation flickered in my stomach and sparked along my skin. That prickle turned to a quiver, then a shudder, then I had to bite my lip because my legs started to shake and my thighs were going numb.

"Oh my God," I whispered. "I think... JP, I'm gonna come."

"Oh, *yes*," he hissed, lifting his head away from my tits to look up at me. "Fuck yes, Nellie. Do it, babe."

I whimpered, digging my fingernails into his back, clutching him desperately as my mind went as numb as my legs were. It took all the sense I had left for me to pitch forward and bury my face against his shoulder so that when that euphoric wave of release crashed through me, the high-pitched noises I couldn't control were muffled by his skin as I lost the rhythm I'd been riding him at and just let my orgasm decide what my body needed.

"That's it," he murmured, the words barely cutting through the electrifying sensation overwhelming me. "You're doing so good, babe. You're riding it so fucking good."

My eyes slammed shut as the final moment of tense pleasure overtook me, then released, relaxing my body all at once. The shaking in my legs subsided, but they were still numb as the intensity of my orgasm subsided. I tried to keep moving, but it was useless.

"JP," I gasped. "I... I think my legs are asleep."

He laughed, the sound dry and exhilarated all at once. "Fuck yeah, they are."

"I can't... I—"

Words weren't working, so I tried to show him I was having trouble riding him by not riding him.

I mean, I tried to. It wasn't like I just flopped against him and held still. I tried to roll my hips, tried to resume what I'd been doing, but it wasn't working. JP made a soft noise, then shifted so he could tighten his arms around me.

"Hold on, babe," he murmured.

For what, I wanted to ask, but before I could, JP slid down on the bed a bit, bent his knees, and started fucking me.

Really fucking me.

God, I hoped Anne-Marie and Remy were distracted, because JP's dick was pushing air out of my lungs, making loud, gasping noises that I couldn't control. My body crashed against his, my tits bouncing against his face as he took over. I reached forward, bracing one hand against the headboard in case he let go of me because I was pretty sure if he did, I'd fly off his lap. The sound of our skin slapping together filled my ears, underscored by the sound of JP panting beneath me, his breath hot against my cleavage.

"Nell," he said after what felt like ages and at the same time, felt like no time at all. "I'm close. Is it okay to—"

"No!" I gasped, suddenly alarmed. "Not in me."

"Where do you want—"

"Come in my mouth."

Now, I think JP was trying to be responsible.

I *think* he was warning me that he was *getting* close, not that he was literally about to come. But for some reason, telling him to come in my mouth made things a lot more imminent.

"Oh, *shit*," he groaned. "Fuck, I'm—"

His arms loosened and he almost shoved me off the bed in his haste to get me off his lap. I caught myself and lurched forward, diving down to take his cock in my mouth.

"*Fuck*!" he grunted again, and his fingers twisted in my hair as he erupted.

Whenever I'd gone down on Adrian, he would barely move. He'd let me control the pace and the depth and everything. Maybe because blowjobs with him never lasted longer than a few minutes, or maybe because he didn't know what to do.

JP, on the other hand, shoved his dick down my throat.

And that should have bothered me. I should have been upset by him using my mouth the way he did.

But I wasn't.

He didn't mean to choke me. He wasn't pushing my head down intentionally or holding me in place because he wanted to. I knew that, even as he thrust into my throat and I gagged around him.

I knew it because he couldn't even control the volume of his voice. Because he'd admonished me playfully, telling me to be quiet so Anne-Marie wouldn't hear us, but couldn't hold back the desperate gasps and groans as his cock pulsed and he emptied a load of cum directly down my throat. I knew, even as tears sprung in my eyes, that he hadn't purposely lost control.

Not when he was making earnest, uninhibited, insanely erotic noises like that.

He held my head against his pelvis until he was spent, his grip loosening as he collapsed against the headboard. Pulling away, I sat back on my knees, heaving for breath as I ran the back of my hand across my mouth, wiping away the spit that had leaked out and onto my chin.

"Fuck," JP said, his voice worried as he forced himself to sit up again. "Did I hurt you?"

I tried to tell him it was okay, but the words came out as a cough that I made worse by trying stifle it.

"*Shit*," he swore, reaching forward and pulling me towards him. Panicked eyes searched mine as he lifted a tender hand to my cheek, cupping it carefully in a strange juxtaposition to the way he'd just shoved his cock down my throat. "I'm so—I didn't mean... Fuck. I'm so fucking sorry, Nellie."

"It's fine," I finally managed to say, brushing my hand under my eyes to wipe away the tears there. "I'm—" I stopped to cough again. "—I'm fine."

"No," he said. "That was horrible of me. I'm so sorry. You said to come in your mouth and I just—"

"It's okay."

I tried not to sniffle as my nose watered. JP winced and brought me in close to him, wrapping his arms around me.

"It's not okay," he said. "I'm sorry. I didn't—"

"JP, stop ruining it," I said, my voice hoarse.

He paused. "What?"

Finally, my throat seemed to clear. "It was hot."

He stared at me. "It... what?"

"It was pretty fucking hot," I said. "I mean, you can't deny that."

He held my gaze for a moment more, then started laughing. I couldn't help but smile as another warm sensation spread through my body, though it was in my chest this time and had nothing to do with an imminent orgasm.

"Shit," he said. "Don't tell me I gave you a choking kink or something. I'd hate to ruin your life like that."

I scoffed. "Please. Like I'd let someone like *you* ruin my life."

He raised his eyebrows and for a moment, I thought I'd insulted him. Which was fair. JP and I didn't have the kind of relationship where I could make fun of him like that.

We didn't have *any* kind of relationship.

But that wasn't why he was giving me that look.

"You won't again, you mean," he said.

It was my turn to raise my eyebrows. "What do you mean, *again*? When did you ruin my life?"

JP's mouth twitched. "Not me. Someone *like* me. Some asshole made up a story about you because he didn't deserve you and you let it stop you from going after what you wanted."

He wasn't anything like Adrian. I wasn't sure why he thought he was. But that wasn't what I focused on.

"Oh, of course," I said. "I should just go out and sleep around next time, then?"

"I mean, yeah."

I made an incredulous noise and JP burst out laughing.

"If you wanna sleep around, sleep around," he said. "Don't let other people make you feel ashamed about it. You're better than that."

I blushed, though I wasn't sure if it was because I was embarrassed or flattered or what. JP chuckled when I didn't say anything.

"There's nothing wrong with liking sex, Nellie. And frankly, you *should* be encouraged. Because you are just—" He made an unintelligible noise, shaking his head in appreciation. "You are so fucking good in bed. Like, it would be a disservice to society if you *didn't* fuck around with as many people as possible, so—"

"Are you serious?" I asked, staring at him in horror.

He laughed again. Like, *hard*. His face turned red and he shook his head.

"You're a bastard," I muttered.

"I'm just telling it like it is," he said as he tried to control his laughter. "You're an absolute natural, babe."

I glared at him. "Don't call me babe."

He smirked. "You didn't seem to mind it when I—"

And then we both heard a door open.

"Nellie?" Anne-Marie called from the hallway.

JP and I didn't so much as look at each other. I shot out of his arms and he bolted into action, pulling on his jeans as I lunged across the room and wrapped myself in his robe again. I glanced in the mirror, flattening my hair as best I could and hoping I could pass off the flush on my cheeks as embarrassment.

"Nellie, where are you?" Anne-Marie said as JP pulled his shirt on.

"In here!" I answered, snatching the hairdryer and my makeup bag off JP's dresser.

"In... where?" she called, confusion in her voice.

"Nellie—" JP said.

I whirled towards him, clutching the hairdryer to my chest.

"Don't tell anyone," I whispered. "Please?"

He blinked, then nodded. I turned around and yanked the bedroom door open to see a startled Anne-Marie standing in the hall.

"What are you doing in Jean-Paul's room?" she asked, frowning. "And in his... robe?"

"I left my clothes in your room before you kicked me out," I said, keeping my voice as flat as I could.

She burst out laughing. "Oh, *no*! I'm so sorry, *chérie*!"

"It's fine." I didn't so much as glance behind me before swinging the door shut. "Let's get ready to go out."

Chapter Thirteen
The Last Time

"Eleanor! There you are! We were worried *sick*!"

I stared at Brayleigh. She smirked at the horrified betrayal on my face as her voice echoed through the foyer, the front door closing behind me with a resounding thud. Seconds later, the sound of my dad's footsteps started towards us.

"You said you'd tell him!" I hissed.

"Oops," she whispered, then returned to the slightly-too-loud volume she'd been using before to make sure my dad would hear her. "Of course we were worried! We didn't know you were staying out all night. But apparently, neither did you. Is this dress new?"

She motioned at my outfit, which was the dress Anne-Marie had lent me to go to the bar the previous night.

"Eleanor," my dad said before I could respond, his voice cold. "Where have you been?"

"At the Marchands'," I said. "Anne-Marie and I—"

"The Marchands'," he repeated, his voice crisp. "That is why when I spoke to Jean-Luc an hour ago, he told me you were not anywhere in his house?"

Oh, *fuck*.

"I was supposed to be at the Marchands'," I said. "But I—"

"And at what point were you going to inform me of that?" he snapped.

"I asked Brayleigh to tell you, but she must have forgotten." I was almost surprised that he let me finish my sentence. "And if I could just explain—"

"It had better be a good explanation," Brayleigh said. "Considering you're lying about telling me any of this."

I looked at my dad, my jaw clenched. He stared back, then glanced at Brayleigh.

"Go wait in my office," he said.

She looked confused. "What?"

He didn't repeat himself. She seemed to think he would, then finally swallowed hard before turning and walking down the hall with her shoulders back and her chin held up.

"I was supposed to be at the Marchands'," I said once she was gone. "But I wanted to leave the bar earlier than Anne-Marie did. So I went to Celine's place and slept on her couch."

"Mmm," my dad said, unconvinced. "And the reason you backtracked on your story was...?"

"I didn't backtrack," I said. "I didn't sleep well last night and I thought you wanted to know, like, everything. So I started with the Marchands' because that was the first place I went yesterday." I pretended to stifle a yawn. "Then Anne-Marie and I met up with Celine and a few other friends. We went to Vivre, then Club Lumina, then I went back to Celine's apartment because I thought Brayleigh told you she'd asked me to stay out of the house so I wouldn't interrupt your dinner party."

"Did she?" my dad said, and his voice had gotten even colder, though it didn't seem to be directed at me.

I nodded. "Otherwise I would've sent you a text. I always text if I'm not coming home, Dad."

Which was true.

Up until the night before, anyway.

But somehow, I convinced him. Probably because my dad was about to go break things off with Brayleigh and was distracted. Honestly, it was a shock that he finally nodded and allowed me to go up to my room to shower and get ready for brunch, especially because it felt like the fact that I hadn't been at Anne-Marie's *or* Celine's was flashing across my forehead like a neon sign.

Or, more accurately, like a burgundy hickey under my left ear.

When I was in tenth grade, Anne-Marie had told me that Clinton Thibault, who had been a sleazy asshole even when I'd known him before I moved to Toronto with my mom, had gotten a girl at another school pregnant.

"She is not keeping it," Anne-Marie had said as we sat in my dad's living room. "That's what my friend who goes to her school said. I asked Jean-Paul but he says he did not know her, which makes sense, I suppose, since she's our age and he's been graduated for a while now. But I don't know if she's not keeping it as in she's putting it up for adoption or if she's not keeping it as in having an—"

"What are we discussing here, girls?"

Both of us jumped as my dad entered the room. His eyebrows were furrowed, a suspicious and almost disgusted look on his face. I flushed red, partly because he'd overheard us and mostly because my dad was the kind of person who believed a bride shouldn't wear white on her wedding day if she wasn't a virgin.

But Anne-Marie seemed blissfully unaware of that.

"Clinton Thibault got a girl pregnant," she said, her voice almost gleeful. "I was just updating Nellie on the situation."

My dad's mouth tightened. "You seem quite pleased about this."

"Oh, no," Anne-Marie said, shaking her head. "I just—"

But my dad didn't let her finish.

"It's horribly irresponsible," he said. "A girl of your age, unmarried, falling pregnant? She could have ruined both of their lives. The level of irresponsibility—"

"But Mr. Belanger," Anne-Marie said, not noticing that my dad's eyes practically turned red as she interrupted him. "She said Clinton was using a condom but took it off without her knowing. That's why she's so upset, because she thought they were being safe but he—"

"And if she hadn't decided to whore around in the first place, it wouldn't have been a problem," my dad said. "Now, if you are done sharing entirely inappropriate stories, I believe your mother was asking for you to return home, Ms. Marchand."

When I returned to Toronto, I told my mom both what had happened to that poor girl and what my dad had said about it.

"Says the man who has a new girlfriend every fucking time you visit him," she spat, her cheeks flaring red with anger. "What a goddamn hypocrite."

"Maybe he's not doing that with them," I said.

Mom gave me a *Look*. "Sweetie, your father's mantra might as well be 'Do as I *say* I do, not *as* I do.'"

A few days later, she picked me up from school early and took me to the doctor to get a prescription for the pill.

"What am I supposed to do with them when I visit Dad?" I asked, flipping the packet of pills over in my hand. "I have to take it every day, but he'll be pissed if he sees me with these."

"Hide them in a box of tampons," she replied. "It's just for a couple more years, anyway. Then you never have to see your father again and it won't matter."

Except obviously, I was still seeing my dad.

Which meant that he could never find out. Not about the pill or the hickey or any of it.

Which meant that Anne-Marie could absolutely *never* know the truth.

Partly because if she found out, JP and I would be standing in the Notre Dame Basilica before we knew it, clad respectively in a tux and approximately eighty-six pounds of taffeta and lace, both of us objecting loudly as the priest announced anyone opposed to our union should speak now or forever hold their peace.

But mostly, if Anne-Marie found out, I might as well have just put that information on a billboard by the highway myself. *Everyone* would find out if Anne-Marie found out, and although it wouldn't be much worse than if just my dad found out, it would still be worse.

Even my mom would be livid. Not about me having sex. She was much cooler than my dad in that respect. But if she found out that I'd had sex with JP Marchand...

I mean, she knew the Marchands. She'd been their neighbour too, up until she divorced my dad. And while she didn't *hate* them the way she hated my dad, she wasn't exactly their biggest fan.

"Jean-Luc Marchand is more full of shit than the solid gold toilet he has in his bathroom," she'd said about Anne-Marie's dad more than once. I didn't think the Marchands actually had a solid gold toilet, but that wasn't the point.

And while she didn't have quite the same vitriol towards Della, she scoffed at any mention of her, mostly because Della was ingrained in the high society types of social circles my dad wanted my mom to be involved in and my mom had adamantly refused. Her feelings for Anne-Marie, who had visited me in Toronto once, were slightly better. Even though she thought Anne-Marie was a "silly rich girl," she thought she had potential.

"She's smart," Mom had said. "She's playing the game, but she's playing with her own rules."

I had a feeling that opinion wouldn't extend to JP, though. Even as a kid, everyone had known he would follow in his dad's footsteps. Which meant he'd go to law school, take over his dad's firm, inherit more money than any one person would know what to do with, marry some beautiful woman who would ingrain herself in those high society social circles, and start the cycle all over again.

Regardless, she knew the Marchands. Which meant the fallout of her finding out would be two-fold: she'd be livid I'd lied about cutting my dad out of my life like she thought I should, and she'd be disappointed I gave it up to a guy like JP Marchand.

So no one could know about this. And that was okay. It wasn't like JP would have been interested in anything more than our clandestine hookup. He was twenty-three and almost finished law school. I was eighteen and just starting university. Those five—well, technically four, but it was almost five—years between us were a lot. We might as well be from two different planets in terms of what we'd have in common.

And that was fine. It wasn't like I thought there would be a next time or even wanted one. There were plenty of other guys I could have sex with instead.

And I did.

Starting that night.

"Oh, what about him?" Anne-Marie shouted over the music at Club Lumina.

I looked in the direction she was pointing. At a table near the dance floor was an admittedly good-looking guy with sandy blonde hair who was wearing a button-up shirt the same shade of blue as JP's eyes.

"I don't like blondes," I shouted back.

She gave me an unimpressed look. "You are blonde, *chérie*."

I lifted my glass to my lips. "I said what I said."

"It's like you don't even want to fall in lust at first sight with one of these fine men," she teased.

And that's what it was. Just teasing. Because I'd told her how many times by that point that I didn't want to have sex with some random guy for my first time.

But it wasn't my first time anymore.

"Ladies," said a smooth voice. I turned to see a man with a boyish face and warm white skin grinning as he leaned in, beer on his breath and glazing his eyes. "What're two nice girls like you doing in a place like this?"

I raised my eyebrows at him. "That's the best you've got?"

The man blinked and let out a startled laugh. "What?"

I tilted my head to the side in amusement. "That's your best pickup line? 'What's a nice girl like you doing in a place like this'? I'm not even worth a more original pickup line to you?"

The guy laughed again. "You totally are. I'm just so distracted by your stunning eyes that I can't think of anything else."

I twisted my mouth to the side. "That's better. But I was kinda hoping you'd compliment my beautiful body and ask if I'd hold it against you."

He flicked his eyes down, then back up, amusement on his face. "I just didn't think a gorgeous creature like you would let me lick her shoes, let alone hold her body against me. But I would be fucking honoured if you'd dance with me, babe."

It should have bothered me. It had bothered me all through my last year of high school, when I'd been called a slut and a hoe more times than I could count. I knew being with one guy didn't make me a hoe, but sleeping with two different guys in one day? I was sure there'd been a rumour or three about that very situation.

But all I could think about was what it was like to sit on JP's cock.

How tight I'd been around him. How full I'd felt. How hard I'd come with someone inside me like that.

How fucking good it was.

And how much I wanted to feel that again.

JP had a point. There was nothing wrong with enjoying sex. And God, had I fucking enjoyed it.

He'd made me feel like there was nothing wrong with wanting sex. Nothing wrong with it not having to be some big, life-changing, emotionally charged moment.

But there *was* something wrong with letting the rumour Adrian started stop me from doing what I wanted. With letting what other people thought about sex change how I lived my life and how I felt about myself.

So I pretended to think for a moment, then finished the last sip of my drink.

"Well, fine," I said, holding my hand out so he could help me up. "But don't call me babe."

"What should I call you instead, then?" he asked.

"My name's Nellie."

"Nellie," he repeated. "Nice to meet you. I'm Insert-Name-Here."

I never could remember what his name was. Hell, I don't even know if I heard him say it over the music or if I just purposely refused to remember it. It didn't seem to matter that much. When Anne-Marie came over after my dad and I went for brunch and I told her that I didn't know the name of the guy I'd ended up going home with the previous night, she squealed.

"I am so proud of you, *chérie*!" she said, wiping fake tears from her eyes. "After everything, you got over those rumours and did what *you* wanted." She sniffled and a moment later, the tears weren't so fake. "I really, truly am proud of you."

"Thanks," I said, trying not to laugh.

She wiped her face again, then clapped her hands and leaned forward, speaking in a conspiratorial whisper. "I want *all* the details. Was it any good?"

I grimaced and her face fell.

"Oh no, *chérie*. What happened?"

"At one point, I think he thought he was supposed to stick it in my belly button."

She nearly fell off my bed as she shrieked with laughter. "He did *not*!"

I shrugged helplessly. "Either that or he confused my stomach and my crotch. And I know I don't have a flat tummy or anything, but they definitely don't look all that similar."

"Ohmigod," she said, still giggling. "I'm so sorry, Nellie. I can't believe you ended up with another virgin."

"Oh, he wasn't a virgin," I said.

"That's even worse. So did he... I mean, did he ever make it out of your belly button? Or are you still technically—"

"No, he did," I said. "I got on my hands and knees and told him to try from behind."

Her mouth dropped open. "That was brave of you, considering he was having so much trouble finding the right hole. Weren't you scared he'd... you know..."

"I told him if he even put it near my butthole, I'd pull his dick between his legs and fuck his own ass with it," I said.

She blinked at me. "Oh... wow. And he still, uh... wanted to have sex?"

"He thought it was funny." I shrugged. "And he didn't put it in my butt, so I didn't have to prove I was serious."

She cackled again. "You are crazy, *chérie*. So he got it in?"

"Eventually."

"And?"

"And... then he took it out... and then put it in again."

She rolled her eyes. "And then took it out."

"Yep."

"And put it in and took it out and put it—"

"Nope," I said. "Just the two times."

"Wait, what?"

"In, out," I said. "And then in. And then he stayed there for a while because he was busy filling up the condom and then he took it out."

"Ohmigod," she said. "He only lasted—"

"Two thrusts." I nodded. "Apparently all that belly button action got him closer to the edge than he'd thought."

That time she really did fall off my bed as she laughed, though I think she was purposely trying to be dramatic. Still, I couldn't help but giggle along with her.

"Oh my God," she said, wiping tears from her cheeks a few moments later. "I am so sorry, *chérie*. I hope he did not turn you off sex forever. It gets better, I promise. Much, *much* better."

If I hadn't had sex with JP first, maybe things would've been different. If he hadn't fucked me the way he did, if I hadn't made him lose control with my words and my mouth and felt the thrill of him submitting to that primal, aggressive part of him that held my head against his pelvis as he came down my throat, if I hadn't come so hard that my legs had gone numb and my mind had gone blank and stars had pricked in my eyes...

If the story I told Anne-Marie and anyone else I talked to about my first time was true, maybe I would've been turned off sex for a while, at least.

But I already knew how good it could be.

JP said he didn't want to ruin my life, and even though he'd been joking, he kind of *had*. Like, my first time having sex had been so good that I couldn't help comparing everyone else to him. And maybe if things had been different, I would've told him that. Maybe I would've told him he'd set me on a path to find sex as good as my first time had been with him.

Maybe if my dad wasn't so prudish and my mom wasn't so desperate to keep me away from my dad, I would've stopped the next day when I was packing the last of my things into my car so I could move to Ottawa.

Maybe I would've acknowledged that I saw JP standing on the driveway next door.

Maybe I would've done something other than turn red as he saw me and raised his eyebrows.

Maybe I wouldn't have gotten into my car and driven away.

But that was the last time I'd seen JP.

The Story Continues

Get JP's point-of-view in the exclusive bonus epilogue!
Find it here: **geni.us/bndbonus**

Then grab your copy of Kiss Me If You Can, the first book in the If You Can
series: **geni.us/kmiyc**

En Francais, S'il Vous Plait

Or, a List of Quebecois Words and Phrases In This Book

As the If You Can series is set partially in Montreal, there are several Francophone and bilingual characters. For practicality's sake, the book is mainly written in one language and it may be noted in the text whether a character was speaking French or English. However, there are points where specific words or phrases are kept in French. For those who would like a translation, they are listed on the following page.

Cherie: endearment, like "dear" or "darling"

Tabarnak: similar to "fuck" as an expression of anger/surprise/annoyance

Ma fille ange: my angel girl or my angel daughter

Oui: Yes, can be used as a phone greeting

Merci: thank you

Ayoye: an exclamation, "wow!"

Salopard: bastard

Tas de merde: piece of shit or pile of shit

Une pute anglophone: an anglophone (English-speaking) whore

Pouffiasses: derogatory, like "slag" or "bimbo"

Fuckboys: Fuckboys

Les Bleus: The Blues

Vivere: To live/be alive

Monsieur: sir or mister

Waouh: whoa or wow

Putain de merde: exclamation, like "holy shit" or "fucking hell" or "what the fuck." Literally means "whore of shit."

C'est quoi ça, tabarnak: similar to "What the fuck." Literally, "What is that [insert *sacres** here]"

Mon dieu: My god

Arrête d'essayer de me contrôler: Stop trying to control me

*Sacres are Quebec-specific swear words related to Catholicism and are considered similar to the word "fuck" in terms of severity

Acknowledgments

I never know how to start these things. It feels like I should intro it but really, I just want to say thank you to a bunch of people. So here are those people.

To my beta readers, proof readers, sounding boards, and cheerleaders: Nora, Jason, Charlie, GG, John, Lisa, Sipho, and Lauren: thank you for helping turn this book from a rough draft to a real book.

Nazarea Andrews from Inkslinger PR has been an absolute blessing over the past months - thank you for helping me stay sane and making life so much easier for me!

Paul M, Kevin Matheny, PM, KJ, MidNyt, RP, Alex, and GW, and all my incredible supporters on Patreon and in my Cheryl's Terrors group - you are amazing people, every single one of you. Thank you for coming along on this journey with me and loving the characters as much as I do!

The vast insanity that is all the family and friends who have been amazing supporters this whole time means I will almost certainly miss someone important if I try to list them all. Please just know I'm so grateful for your support and all that you do. For everyone who has asked for a bookmark or suggested my book to a friend or listened to me blab about something writing related - you make such a difference to me. Thank a million times over.

To my parents, thank you for being there for me and all your encouragement. Mom, a special reminder not to read this book at work like you did with the short story series.

Becca and Rachel, thanks for being amazing friends and supporters. A special shout-out to Pam for picking up my book and being an amazing cheerleader for it.

Cheddar and Pumpkin: woof woof. bark bark. Good girls.

To my wonderful husband: Thank you. Thank you. Thank you. You are and always will be my person.

Join The Chaos

Every hot mess deserves a happy ending.

Get exclusive bonus scenes, short stories, novellas, and more by joining my newsletter: **cherylterra.com/newsletter**

Find even more bonus content, early access to new work, and weekly updates that I sometimes actually do post every week on my Patreon (free tier available!): **patreon.com/cherylterra**

Also By Cheryl Terra

Also By Cheryl Terra

Find all of Cheryl's books at cherylterra.com/stories

Aurora Flats Series

Fate and Fried Chicken

If You Can Series

The Boy Next Door
Kiss Me If You Can
Hold Me If You Can
Keep Me If You Can
Sleigh Me If You Can

Unicorn Confessions Series

The Unicorn Confessions
Unicorn For Sale
Death of a Unicorn

Love Across Canada Series

Get Over It
The Devil Made Me
Runaway
Finding Home

Standalones

When It Rains
Hearts at Play: Special Edition
One Little Question
What Happens In Vegas
Selfish Love
Another Last Call